Killing the ~~**Kardashians**~~

~~*A Satirical Novella of Modern Day Banality*~~

Todd ~~**Houghton**~~

This satirical novella is intended to expose and criticize the United States of America's obsession with celebrities, commercialism, and violence. It is a work of fiction involving real and fictional characters, celebrities, and places. All of the events described in this book are fictitious and solely the work of the author's imagination. No person or company referenced in this book endorses this book or gave permission to be the subject of the author's satire. The book is not intended to incite violence against anyone or any place and is not a call of action to any kind of action whatsoever from the reader. The celebrities being depicted in this novella are done so in jest and thus making the depictions entirely ridiculous and inaccurate.

This satirical novella should only be read by people who have never taken a selfie.

When sociopathy meets stupidity *Keeping Up with the Kardashians* suddenly becomes Killing the Kardashians.

The Stars of Killing the Kardashians:

Eric Ryder: Host — Your Momentary Glamour Messiah aka the Self-Aware Narcissist

Elizabeth Betan: Co-host — Mary Magdalene aka the Girl who Loves Shiny Things

James Ford: Cameraman — Judas Iscariot aka the Predestined Betrayer

The Satirical Guests of Killing the Kardashians:

Kim Kardashian: The Filth aka the Queen of Selfies/Banality

Kourtney Kardashian: The Slop aka the Monotone Mother

Khloe Kardashian: The Pig aka the Bride Who's Never a Wife

Lieutenant Waterman: The Lout aka Keanu Reeves Lover/Henry Rollins look-alike

Ronda: The Girl with the Golden Fists aka the Only Person Eric Fears

Kanye West: The Ghetto Pope aka the Unaware Narcissist/Eric's Evil Twin

Iggy Pop: Michigan's Beloved Son aka the Creator of Everything Cool

"The books that the world calls immoral are books that show the world its own shame."

Oscar Wilde

1

Eric Ryder
Your Momentary Glamour Messiah
Apathy's Lungs
In the Bosom of Apathy, United States of America: Endless Fall of Rome
apathyslovingprince@fuckamerica.com

Apathy: The Child of the United States of America
When You're Yearning for Apathy's Embrace
The Way Out of the United States and to the Decadence of Rome

Dear Apathy:

I guess if you're reading this we're all corpses being raped by the necrophiliac we refer to as social media. In between selfies and drinking Double Mocha Frappuccinos I imagine the plebs will find the time to tweet about all of this. Comments ranging from, "Awesome, I hated the Kardashians!" to, "How can people be so evil? They must be sociopaths." Then finding a comment like, "I didn't like them, but I never wanted them to die." Then finally, "I wish I had thought of it." All these nitwits will then bicker with one another and raise their blood pressure before eating donuts and ice cream. After that they forget the entire thing has happened and order a pizza. Once they're full they'll watch porn that more than likely includes the fantasies of rape and fucking a meth addict who's at the perfect stage of her/his addiction making her/him fashionably thin in the most perfect way possible. After the release they'll wipe their hands on the wall and see what's going on in the world of social media just before bed. They'll find some political bullshit about gun control—after what we've done—and of course have a strong stance on it (be it for or against) then have a meltdown when one person disagrees with them. Now the special children of today are too upset to sleep and stay up all night streaming mindless movies and TV shows. Fuck, now it's 8 AM and time for work. It's time for the special children of today to speed and pass someone who's going too slow. Unfortunately, only 1 percent of these people will die in a wreck. Oh, look, we're at work now. We had to ride the elevator with that person we hate, but whom we pretend to love. How did I get at my desk? Oh, I need to finish this paper work that won't matter when I'm dead. I'm proud of what I've done with my life. If it wasn't for senseless jobs I wouldn't be able to use social media and drink coffee that isn't called coffee and has 5,000 calories per cup. I'm not overweight, that chart is just wrong. If I were that skinny I would be a rail. This gut isn't fat it just shows I have culture. Last night my stomach and I visited Italy, Greece, Mexico, and China. I'm awesome, let me post a picture of my food so you can see it. When I'm done and it's time to defecate I think I might post that, too. Hey, I just started a new trend. I have 100,000 followers now. My life is complete. I think I'll die now. Here lies the vomit of the human species. A beloved son, a fast food connoisseur, and mindless narcissist who accomplished the amazing task of taking over 10 million selfies in his life. God Bless America.

Sincerely,

Eric Ryder

2

So I disembark on the ascendency of my infiniteness. My coruscating eyes drip to the floors of unfound sheath. I stand in a morning recondite from the slumbering scions; ardent in its clasp. Outside the wind we flock; breath of wisp and comely in this hour of lechery.

In other words burn Hollywood and make society choke on the ashes.

And now back to the task at hand. Such a thing. Such a glorious, incandescent thing.

"You know we're not coming out of this alive, right? None of us." Both Elizabeth and James nod as they look at me. "We're making a statement here and it'll ring until the end of mankind," I say. "It'll provoke change." How nice to be able to say this, to mean it, and *know* that it's true.

Elizabeth smiles as she can already taste the blood of our burden. "Fabulous darling."

I turn to James, who is average in almost every aspect of his life. Yet, there's an underlining prickly quality to him that tatters his very existence. "Their stupidity has forced us to do this. We're the saviors that society needs."

James looks unsure. I have no idea if he's ever had a moment of certainty in his life. Quickly he glances at Elizabeth (always needing her approval) and then back to me. "We can do this, Eric."

We went over this at least fifty fucking times. "James, what did I tell you before? Stop talking. You're the cameraman."

"I'm sorry."

"What the fuck did I just say? Are you mentally fucked?"

As usual, Elizabeth—the unhinged referee—steps in to calm me down. ."Mr. Ryder, now isn't the time to get onto James. He's our baby boy." Elizabeth pinches James's face the way a loving grandmother would.

James tries to hide his elation over feeling Elizabeth's flesh on his face. He loves these moments. Longs for them. I remember the first time I realized what he was after. I know James and I know he still thinks about the first time he truly found her scent on his clothes. He had made sure to sit right next to her on the couch and only occasionally leaning against her. He had to wrap himself in the zeal of her lace. It was just enough to be able to smell her for later that night. The blade slips to the nails…

I do my best to gather myself. "You're right, just make sure you're doing your job, James. Elizabeth and I will do the rest."

James gives a thumbs up.

I look at them both carefully. Mostly James, to make sure he won't try and back out of this. Elizabeth will die by my side and even finds the idea of it romantic. "They will cry, they will beg, and they'll do anything to get out of this," I say. "You're certain you won't let them off the hook?"

Elizabeth can feel herself bathing in the soft ivy of their screams. "I'll let them off the hook after I stick it in them a few times."

James nods and gives another thumbs up.

A slight smirk finds its way onto my face before we walk down the entryway and out of the mansion.

While waiting on me, Elizabeth is skipping around the living room of the Kardashian mansion while holding two of her favorite knives. She looks like she's just walked out of a Gothic novel illustrated by a graphic artist. Catherine from *Wuthering Heights* meets Harley Quinn. She is as vicious as she is comely.

Meanwhile, I'm making my way upstairs to find the Kardashian sisters. I almost laugh at how terrible this mansion looks. If I were this rich I would create a home that feels like I'm in the bosom of *Judith Beheading Holofernes* while in the skin of *Narcissus*. Who doesn't love Caravaggio? Anyway, I continue with my voyage of ruination. I should mention that I'm tall with an angular face (high cheekbones/sunken cheeks—my contours are fucking brilliant.). I look like a mix of Dorian Gray and Alex from *A Clockwork Orange*. 19th century England meets futuristic dystopian society. I'm a fashionable man who is always properly dressed. I also make sure to keep my body fat percentage between 6 and 8 percent so I always look my best. My diet consists of spinach, blueberries, lean meats, and water. I make sure to lift weights sparingly. Just enough to maintain my weight and have the most desirable body fat percentage. The last thing I want is to look like a Neanderthal and be disgusting and bulky. Idiots like that are the male equivalent of the female bimbo with breast implants, an awful tan that only people with a low IQ could possibly like, and bleached blonde hair. Yes, Elizabeth and I have white hair, but I'm an artist and I'm a natural blond. Elizabeth is a natural blonde, too. My family is all from Friesland and it's in my genetics. Elizabeth's family is from England. She might be from England, actually. She does have an accent, but so do I when I feel like having one. So it might be for show. I'm not entirely sure. But anyway, the hair color suits our skin tone. So fuck off. Oh, one other thing since I know that there will be stupid fucks who noticed I used both blond and blonde and are probably having a seizure over it, so allow me to explain it to you. I know 99 percent of North Americans are fucking idiots (Canadians included) so it's kind of mandatory. Blond is used for men and blonde is used for women. If there is a group (with both sexes) they're referred to as blondes. It's of French etymology and that's how it works. I believe Anglo-French to be exact, but I could be wrong. Did you learn something? Good, now go and text or Tweet or whatever it is morons do today. Make sure to destroy the English language in the process, too. You wouldn't be a good North American if you didn't. After that get your exercise by playing some weird Japanese game where you find Peekaboo or whatever it's called. I mean, it's only meant for children between the ages of 5 and 12, but I'm glad you're getting your exercise. Maybe later you can do some arm toning with Nintendo. Anyway, I lost my original point so let me try and find it. Oh yes, not being a Neanderthal on my part and Elizabeth not being a disgusting Hollywood harlot. I expect Elizabeth to stay as slender as I am and she never lets me down. She also has perfect fair skin untouched by a fucking tanning bed and her breasts are small like they should be for her frame. To put it simply we're flawless. To destroy the simplicity by rape of complexity... we're a perfect Victorian couple in the 21st century. Envy us with your disposable skin.

On the second floor I find three bedrooms with their doors closed. On the doors there are three signs that read as, the Filth, the Slop, and the Pig. I decide to choose the door for the Filth. I'm of course assuming this is Kim (I often confuse the three). I open the bedroom door and looks around the lavish and horribly decorated room. There are pictures of Kim Kardashian all over the room. You can't see any of the walls because they're covered in selfies. I find myself smirking again because Kim is sleeping in a bed that looks like something a little girl would have. I walk in softly, put my hand over her mouth, and point the gun at her head.

"Allow me to introduce myself."

As Kim's eyes widen in fear the canvas of my inquisition betrays the sallowness of my heart. I feel the urge to string her neck in the harps of the chorus. However, a cantata can be just as beautiful as a sonata. Still, I can't but help imagine how beautifully her blood would stain the Egyptian sheets. Calmly I gather myself and I pull out duct tape and put it over Kim's mouth. Then I flip her over and tape her hands and feet together.

3

So then, here it is and here we are. We're face to face with reality TV's most idiotic sisters. Amazingly enough, they're even more unattractive and disgusting in person. The only appealing thing about them is the fact they're tied up and their mouths are taped shut. It's a moment I've waited so long for. It's one of those things that really puts your life in perspective. I find myself thinking about all the times Elizabeth and I would text prostitutes and offer them outrageous amounts of money for unprotected sex. We'd send them on an absurd journey telling them we missed an exit (to the shitty motel) and we'd be there soon. We always found a way to get them to go to the wrong parts of the city late at night. We would laugh and fuck after with the thought of them being decapitated by violent creatures. I know what you're thinking… how awful. I don't know the struggles they've been through. Well, it's as simple as this. They're fucking junkies who will always crave that high they once had. Even if they become clean they'll always yearn for it. They're reprehensible cunts. It's pathetic to make excuses for them. That's the terrible thing about technology and the way we've gotten away from the basics. What the fuck is natural selection now? Now we have idiots with bad immune systems breeding with bitches who have low IQs. Why? All because some douche bag social nitwit is good with computers? Send them into the wild for a month without supplies and see what they become. Now we coddle these people and come up with fancy terms for them and have to treat them like they're special. It isn't their fault! I don't care if it's their fault. Fucking kill them and be done with it. In a century mankind will be better off because of it. Now, don't get me wrong. I don't want us to go back to living like our ancestors did centuries ago. I love the finer things in life. In fact, I demand the finer things in life, but I could have survived then if I'd had to. That's the point and so many people today never could have. Just because we don't live like that anymore doesn't mean we need to weaken our species.

Anyway, where was I? Oh yes, the girls Kim, Khloe, and Kourtney are all tied to chairs in the living room. As I look at Kim I can't help but find a smirk dance across my face. I still remember writing a letter to her after the robbery in Paris. I was concerned with how she might be feeling after the ordeal. I thought it would be a kind gesture to write her a letter and attempt to help her. Would you care to read it? Yes, of course you would. It would be your pleasure. Here it is, dear reader.

Eric Ryder
Your Momentary Glamour Messiah
The Blossoming Discharge of Narcissistic Thoughts
Hollywood, California
10/17/2016

Kim Kardashian
The Filth
Kardashian Enterprises: Rotting Society's Minds One Selfie at a Time
Strumpet Ave. Next to Marilyn Monroe's Fat Face Just South of Fuck
Reality TV
Some Shit Place in California

Dear Kim Kardashian,

Oh my stars, Kimmy. I just heard about the situation you went through in Paris. I'm so sorry about all of it. If I were there with you I would hug you and sing you songs by Hootie and the Blowfish, Ryan Adams, Train, John Mellencamp, and the Dead Kennedys. I don't even know what the fuck I mean by that, but oh well. Back to your awful ordeal. I guess it would make too much sense to ask the question what kind of nitwit carries almost 10 million dollars in tawdry jewelry with them? Certainly, so I won't do that. I'll ask a better question. What kind of nitwit spends almost 10 million dollars on tawdry jewelry? You're not Marie fucking Antoinette. LOL LOL LOL! I love texting and I forgot that I wasn't texting, sorry. I mean, there are kids in other countries taken from their homes and are brainwashed and forced to go back to rape and kill their mothers and sisters. But, hey, I'm glad you're okay. I'm so pleased this was all over the news and the reporters didn't just roll their eyes and say, "what kind of moron would spend that much on jewelry anyway?" Then go to a real story. We wouldn't be the United States of Motherfucking Endless Vapidity of America if we did that. But dear, please get better soon because we miss seeing you on TV or whatever stupid website people watch shit on now. Even your problems are superb, Kimberly. Fighting with your sister about using her backyard for a birthday party for your child, how to make 20,000 dollars per Tweet instead of a mere 10,000, and of course finding a way to silence someone who mocks you because they're employed by the same company as you. These are *real* problems and I'm so pleased our country realizes this and caters to these issues.

Anyway, now that I've expressed how happy I am that you're okay after the Paris fiasco. I must say it has been such a pleasure watching you on your brilliant TV show. To think, I didn't even know that your show existed until Elizabeth insisted I watch an episode a couple months ago. Suddenly, my life feels complete. I think it's only fitting that more people in our country know who you are than Sylvia Plath. I don't think Capitalism would have it any other way. Why should artists be celebrated or respected in any fashion? We should celebrate those who have found one of the endless cracks in Capitalism. Christ, you're the most impressive of all the Capitalists in my mind. You're literally famous for being famous. I love it. I truly do. You're a modern day Marilyn Monroe. Seriously, too. Shall I go over the reasons why? Marilyn had a complete lack of talent for acting. You have that, darling. Marilyn was fat and completely boring looking. You're right there with her on that. Marilyn was also the Queen of Abortions. You're the Queen of Raping Minds of the Youth. That's one area Marilyn has you beat, though. If she really did have a dozen or so abortions as some reports claim it's better than what you're doing. Marilyn at least had the decency to put the poor things out of their misery by never having to be raised by her. You're the metaphorical rapist to our society. You aren't killing anything other than the chance of intelligent thought. You rape minds and force your victims to live on with this pain. It's awful, really. As one of your victims I feel the need to tell you how I feel about it all. That's why I'm writing this to you, dear. As a victim I wish you would abort yourself. Maybe you could televise it and you could use the money to do meth as a walking abortion. I would personally enjoy watching you scratch yourself thinking that there are bugs underneath your skin. A walking abortion addicted to meth. If that isn't the American Dream then nothing is. But, remember to tweet your first meth experience and if you're feeling really like an American cliché try heroin, too. You can take a selfie of yourself injecting heroin in your arm for the first time while smoking meth and trying to abort yourself for the second time. Use a hanger and fish around in yourself and see what you have hiding in there. Probably 80 percent of society's minds. Hey, that gives me an idea for a new product for you. If you want to show Marilyn how it's done, then this is what you should do. You should have several men impregnate you and then have abortions. After each abortion you take whatever is left and then mix it with wine, face cream, or whatever else. You can call it Kim's Abortion Line. You can have several men on TV with you and let the people vote who's going to donate for your next abortion. The people should always be involved that's my philosophy. At the very least I hope you at least consider what I've mentioned because it's important for you to know I only have your best interest at heart. Anyway, Kim. I have to get back to body shaming fat women by sending them away once they take their clothes off in front of me. After that they can cry and blame me for being overweight or not accepting them for having a poor diet and not taking care of themselves. Then calling me a "hater" whatever the fuck that is. After all, why would anyone want to take care of themselves? Silly idea. I'm happy society became so civilized that we can now eat terrible things that ruin our skin and make us fat fucks and pretend everyone is equal when they're not. Well, thanks again for your time, Kim. Remember, when you're in need of a friend I will always be here for you.

Sincerely,

Eric Ryder

     I laugh a little thinking about this letter. Such a simple time and everything was just a dream then. But it's here now and it's right in front of me. So let us continue.
     The room looks like it was decorated by someone who never had any money, but was suddenly given an endless amount to buy whatever they want. If they were to make a bulimic doll that vomits glitter and semen it would look like the Kardashian home.

Elizabeth smiles while looking at the Kardashians. James prepares the laptop and camera to film the show. I'm getting ready to become the celebrity I've always wanted to be. This is what I've prepared for. The difference is I deserve this fame because I have actual talent and intelligence. So, I let myself decline into the very nature of this torrid effulgence. After all, I want their cries to frame my idyllic listlessness I've yearned for. Let us begin.

"Well, hello there! Welcome to our new show! Killing the Kardashians! We're live from the Hyacinth House. I'm your host Eric Ryder. Unfortunately, it's only going to be one episode because there are only so many Kardashians to kill."

Elizabeth casually skips in front of the camera before speaking. She gives the impression of a deranged child who happened upon an adult body that would then serve as her vessel. "But it will be a long episode and one with a lot to learn. Mainly where the most tender parts are on the human body."

"As you can see we have the Kardashian sisters with us. Don't let the ropes fool you, they are here of their own free will. Their stupidity landed them here. In truth, they asked for this. They begged for it." As I look at them I feel elation in a way I never have before. The closest I've ever been to capturing this before was the time I choked my stepmother. Most people love the look in the eyes of the person they're conquering and I certainly did…but the part I loved the most was feeling the fear in her body. I knew I would never forget it. Her bones screamed with a mockery of bliss that not even her defense mechanisms could bind. It was as if I were raping her entire soul. I knew then that I could have anything or anyone I wanted. I released her, but not out of kindness. I wanted my stepmother to live the rest of her life knowing that I was her savior and I could end her at any point. It was a feeling of beauty I have been searching for again and again. There were only glints before. But now, it's as if I'm glistening in God's teeth. Yes, sooner or later God would bite down and it would all be over. But this Momentary Glamour Messiah will never fade. Hello, Marilyn Monroe. I'm Eric Ryder. Is this throne taken? You're pretty meaty, huh? Oh well.

Elizabeth claps in pure joy as she looks at them, wondering what it would be like to cut into their flesh. "They did beg for it. Before the show they called me to make sure I have three knives. One for each of them."

Elizabeth shows her three knives. Each one has the name of the sisters. The other side of the blade has their nicknames. The Filth for Kim, the Slop for Kourtney, and the Pig for Khloe. Elizabeth can hardly control herself as she looks at Kim. Her flesh is calling to her. She drops the knives for Khloe and Kourtney. Elizabeth's blue eyes find a splendor that only comes from the thought of the theistic sound of carving into human flesh. She controls her urge to laugh so as not to disturb me while I talk. She forces herself to focus on me and just how much she loves me.

"So, we're going to make these vapid individuals pay. But how should they pay and how much?"

"Excellent question, daaaarliing. I think they should pay with blood. The going rate is fifteen liters of blood. The average person who weighs one hundred and fifty pounds has around five liters. I'm not sure they'll have enough." Elizabeth frowns as she thinks about not having enough blood.

Kim tries to talk through the duct tape. Elizabeth notices and walks towards her. She takes the duct tape off of her mouth. "Ouch. Khloe has enough for all of us. Don't worry. You'll be like totally blood rich and stuff."

Elizabeth is elated. "So lovely! Oh my god… you're right. She's huge, she will have enough." Kim smiles and cheers with Elizabeth.

I motion for James to turn the camera back to me. "First, let's see how we ended up here."

Elizabeth steps in front of the camera and makes a playfully stern face while pointing her finger at the camera.

I carefully move Elizabeth out of the shot. She's one you have to keep an eye on or things can get out of control. "When I first saw the show I thought it was a joke of some sort," I said. "I found it really, really funny. Then Lizzie told me it wasn't a joke. I was lost for words."

"It's true, he was. I had to pry them out." Elizabeth pretends to try and pry my mouth open. It's annoying and I walk away from her or this will continue for who knows how long.

"Let me set the scene," I say. "This is a text message Khloe received from Kim after Khloe woke her up an entire hour too early! Play it James!"

James rushes to the laptop and quickly plays the clip from the TV show. "Oh my god! Look at what Kim just sent me in a text."

Kourtney asks Khloe, "Like, what does it say?"

Khloe reads the text. "How fucking dare you. You're such an evil bitch. How spiteful and jealous are you? How Fucking dare you, Khloe. You crossed a major line with me. That shit is not okay. You dumb evil little fucking troll. You have no idea how much I hate you. You're disgusting!"

"Oh my god, is she like serious?"

I stand in front of the camera shaking my head. "Yeah, I know... I couldn't believe it either. After watching that, it, 'like totally occurred to me' that this society is by far the dumbest in the world. Go United States! Excuse me while I drink some kind of coffee that isn't really coffee with enough calories for six meals." Wait, did I already mention that before? I don't give a fuck because it pisses me off so much it should be mentioned twice.

"OMG, like totally get me a cup, please!" Kim squeals.

Elizabeth jumps up and down in front of Kim. "Doesn't it sound so delicious, Kimmy dear?"

"OMG, like you know what's awesome when you're pregnant? Since you're already fat and stuff you can literally have around fourteen thousand calories and you don't get fatter 'cause like once the baby comes out the baby is just fatter. After I get tired of being like not fat and stuff and I'm hungry 'cause not being fat is like you know... hard? I just like to be pregnant and eat all the time and like drink coffee with cake in it and stuff."

Khloe is trying to talk through the tape now too. I rip the tape off as hard as I can. Khloe doesn't seem to notice it should hurt. She is pretty macho. "Stop like talking to them and stuff, Kim!"

Kim looks confused. "Like why and stuff? She's nice. I like her."

"I like you too!" Elizabeth hugs Kim. Kim tries to hug her back, but being tied up she can't figure out how to accomplish it.

I walk back in front of the camera. "Luckily, there is some good news for you internet viewers who are watching. You get to participate! As we pick up more viewers we're going to have a little vote."

Elizabeth's eyes flutter joyously. "It'll be a little vote. But a little vote with tons and tons of fun."

"Yes, so little because most of this society is so goddamn fucking moronic. However, those of you who aren't part of the moron clique get to have some fun."

"I can't wait!"

"Neither can I, Lizzie. However, by noon when enough of the intelligent people in our country have found out about this they're going to be able to take part in it."

"Get your finger clickers ready, daaaahrlings!" Elizabeth operates exclusively in high decibels.

"We didn't name our little show Killing the Kardashians just because it's so catchy!"

Elizabeth and I dance together like we're in a ballroom. It's almost as ridiculous as the Kardashians being allowed to have a TV show. While we dance James puts duct tape back over Kim and Khloe's mouths.

4

I examine the Kardashians who are still tied up. I can't help but laugh at Kim who's trying to talk about through the duct tape. I decide to untie Kim and take the tape off of her mouth. Why not? She's too stupid to even try to escape.

Kim starts to yell. "Like help!"

I laugh again. "Yes, someone help this media whore!"

Elizabeth sits down by Kim and yells with her. "I want to try. Help!"

Kim looks at her in confusion, then decides to help Elizabeth out. "No, you need to go higher."

Elizabeth tries in the most absurd manner possible. "Heeeeeeeeeeeeeelllllllp."

Kim claps in approval. "OMG, so good. Do you like want to be my reality double?"

"Can I cut out your husband's larynx if I do it?"

"We don't own a larynx. I so wanted one as a like guard cat thing, though"

"That's a lynx you imbecile. Now shut the fuck up."

Kim starts to cry a little. "Like why are you so mean and stuff? It's like so mean of you to be mean and stuff. Like haven't you seen this bully commercials and stuff. Like I totally knew a girl in high school who killed herself because someone bullied her on Twitter by saying she smokes cigarettes that aren't like digital and stuff. Then everyone in school brought like those like what are they called? Umm… analog or like VHS or something cigarettes and threw them at her and put them in her locker and stuff."

I look at her completely fucking amazed and I do mean completely fucking amazed. "That's a fascinating story especially since they didn't even have goddamn Twitter when you were in high school. What are you, anyway? Fucking 40? Even I know what VHS is and I'm younger than you. Jesus fucking Christ."

"OMG, shut up! I stopped aging at like 18. So I'm like forever 18 and stuff, okay? Oh and for your FYI Twitter was around when I was in high school. When I want to prove to people I'm still so young looking I go back to school as a senorita…"

Being annoyed and just tired of this I cut her off. "It's senior, idiot."

"Uh, like no. I'm not a guy and stuff so I'm a senorita but Khloe would totally be a senior."

"Fucking seriously?" I shout.

"Anyway, like I was like saying and stuff when I go back as a senorita everyone totally thinks I'm 18 and I'm like the most popular and become the like prom queen and like lose my virginity on prom night. I've lost it like 12 times already. Don't worry I make sure they're like 18 like me because I don't want to get in trouble with that statue law thing."

I feel myself crack a little. My persona is down with the camera off. I scream louder than I have ever screamed in my entire life. "Are you really this fucking dumb or are you acting... even now?"

"Like, I just don't understand. What do you mean?" Kim asks confused as she starts to cry.

I shout again. "Did you not watch the video we just showed? Did you not listen to a single fucking word you just said?"

Kim talks into between sobs. "Yes, I did, didn't I look fab? I mean, like, if your goal was to show how fab I looked and how awesome and what a good speecher I am, then I totally get it."

I giggle in a mocking manner while jumping up and down in front of Kim. I feel myself lose more control in this moment than every frustrating event in my life combined. "Like, like, like, I don't get it! How could someone in our society actually hate me? So it must be you're showing it because you love me like everyone. I mean, I've made millions upon millions being a fatuous media whore!"

Elizabeth gets up from the couch and starts to skip for no reason.

Kim tries to understand, but can't. "I don't understand then! Like, what do you want and stuff?"

I pace for a moment without saying anything. Finally, I calm myself and smile. "I want to bring ballet to the masses," I say. A brilliant line from Freddie Mercury. Even this cunt can't possibly ruin that.

Kim claps. "Oh my God, like that's all you want? I think that's a totally awesome idea. I would go to Church like all the time if they had ballet. Well, if they started at like two in the afternoon I could. Anyway, if that's all you need just let me have my people call your people to write you a check for that. Like, how much will that cost? I mean how much do the ballet arena things cost?"

"What the *fuck* are you talking about? Holy shit! Thank you for answering the question if you're really this dumb or not."

"Like oh my God, I'm just trying to give to Church charities and stuff for you, okay? You don't have to be so like rude and stuff."

No one ever considers rudeness a virtue, and everything thinks courtesy is automatically worthwhile. "So every time you hear someone say Jesus Christ do you assume they're praying?"

Kim looks at me with an almost blank stare. "Uh, duh."

I suppose it's nice that I can still be surprised by things, but I just can't deal with it anymore. "James, tape her mouth shut again."

Elizabeth stops skipping for a moment and looks at Khloe and Kourtney. She takes the tape off of their mouths at the same time. "It's okay, dears!"

Kourtney looks at them and fully realizes the situation she and her sisters are in. "God help us."

This grabs my attention. "God's away at the moment. But don't worry because I'm filling in for him."

Kim's mouth hasn't been taped shut again. "Are you like going to rape us and stuff?"

Elizabeth slaps Kim as hard as she can. "Listen, you valley girl bitch. If he's going to rape anyone it's going to be me." Elizabeth stops and thinks for a moment. "Wait, can you like rape?"

I lied. There are always new lows, but I'm sick of being surprised. "What the fuck, I said this once before, but someone tape her mouth shut. Get on it now, James."

James is annoyed with how I constantly demand things from him. But he knows that's just my personality and does his best to forgive me for it. Nonetheless, he likes me, but acting this way with him on TV is different. Still, he knows I'm just annoyed with the Kardashians and lets it go. He goes over, still filming, to tape Kim's mouth.

I sees Kourtney trying to remove the tape from her hands and I kneel down beside her. "Whatcha doin', dear?"

Kourtney tries not to cry. "I don't want to die and stuff."

I think for a moment before I speak. "Well, dear, I didn't want to see this society go from skyscrapers and fast food to skyscrapers, mineral water, and the Kardashians. We're supposed to get better not worse. However! There is good news. Tell 'em, Lizzie."

Elizabeth frowns. "One of you gets to live."

"That's right, and the viewers will decide."

Kourtney cries. "No, that's like awful."

I put my arm around Kourtney and pull her against my body. "It'll be okay, Kourt. We're going to have tons of fun first."

5

I walk in front of the camera, flamboyant and brilliant. It's clear even Freddie Mercury would be proud. The Kardashians are still tied up on the couch as James turns on the camera.

I'm ready in an instant. My world-charming persona, even while destroying said world, sets in. Well, it's not so much a persona as it's just who I am when the light is on me. It comes very naturally.

"Hello there. Welcome back to Killing the Kardashians, live from the Hyacinth House So, it's almost time for the voting. How many viewers do we have James?"

James quickly checks the computer. "About 20,000 at the moment."

"Did you call the news stations yet?"

"Not yet, Eric."

"Get on it then. But until then we'll give our loyal viewers something else to vote on. They deserve to have some fun until then."

Kim cheers loudly. "OMG, are we like going to the beach and stuff?"

I shake my head, slightly confused. "No."

Kim's eye light up as she thinks she's figured it out. "Oh, I know! To see my plastic surgeon? I so totally need to go up another size with my butt implants."

"Stop fucking talking," I say, annoyed at my sudden lack of composure. We planned this for months and every word I utter is supposed to be perfect. But with them in front of me… it's proving to be extremely daunting. "Do you ever stop talking?" I ask trying to hide my vexation.

"Totally. Like when I get botox the doctor tells me to stop talking or I could mess him up."

Three deep breaths. Three deep breaths. "Okay, then pretend that you're getting botox now."

Kim is excited by this absurd suggestion. "Like oh my god, do you think if I pretend I'm getting it and I imagine that I'll get the same results?"

I can't help but laugh now. I mean… wow. "The mind is a powerful thing, so that could happen."

Kim claps. "OMG, so cool." Kim then motions to show that she isn't going to talk to make sure the imaginary botox will work.

Khloe finally speaks, obviously hungover. "What do you mean by fun?"

"The viewers will have three choices," I say. "That we each pick for one of you. For example I pick for Kim."

Kim forgets that she isn't supposed to talk. "Pick what?"

"Kim, your botox isn't going to work if you talk."

"Oh yeah!" Kim shows she's zipping her lips again.

"For example, for Kim I would pick…" I look at Elizabeth and continue. "Lizzie, cover Kim's ears so she doesn't hear the surprise."

Kim breaks her silence again. "OMG, is it my birthday?"

"Kim, you're messing up your botox."

Kim nods and Elizabeth covers Kim's ears, too.

I smile softly before speaking. "As I was saying. For Kim I would pick she has her butt implants removed."

Kourtney rolls her eyes at me. "Like, a doctor would never do that, duh."

I grin at Kourtney. It's clear she doesn't fully grasp how this entire situation works. I calmly pick up a bag on the floor and pull out a sharp knife. "Well, if a doctor doesn't agree to it then I'm going to torture you on camera until one does. Then, if one still doesn't agree I'll perform the surgery myself."

Kourtney shudders. "You're a psycho."

Elizabeth can't control her smile. "He sure is."

I walk towards Kourtney and pretend that I have compassion for her and the situation she's in with her sisters. "I'm sorry, but this is how it works and it's up to the viewers. Your turn, Lizzie dear."

Elizabeth rubs her hands together. She's been waiting for this day for so long and now it's finally here. "For Khloe I pick that I get to carve 'drunk slut' into her forehead with my knife. See, this one."

I grin. "Brilliant, I love it. James, you're up."

James thinks for a moment. He knew that this was coming and planned out a few different things. Still, he isn't sure what the right way to go about this is. He thinks of me as a brother, but he *loves* Elizabeth. He thinks she's the one for him and he's thought it since the first time he met her. He thinks that I don't love her. He isn't sure I even like her. He thinks I just use her and yell at her all the time. He thinks he will truly appreciate and love Elizabeth if he gets her. That's something I will never do. At least he believes that. But, then he realizes what if he makes Elizabeth mad in the process? Almost everything he has in mind will make Elizabeth angry. He knows he has to do it, though. It's worth the risk. If you don't risk something you're never going to gain anything. He learned that from me. Too bad for him I know what he's up to.

"James, what do you pick?"

"Sorry, Eric. I know now. I pick that Kourtney has to legally marry you."

Elizabeth lets out a hellacious scream. "That's not how it works, James!"

James smirks as Eric pulls Elizabeth aside. "It isn't a big deal. We're all going to die soon, anyway. It's just a way to mock them. You know that you're the only one I love."

Elizabeth glares at James who is now hiding his joy over what's just happened. "Fine," she replies coldly.

The results are in and I look at James. "Well, who's the winner, James?"

James conceals his happiness behind a blank face as he tells me the results. "It looks like you're going to be a married man, Eric."

You can't plan for everything, I suppose. Humanity, cesspool that it is, is a broken system with innumerable variables. "Well, fuck. Get an ordained minister or whatever then."

Elizabeth glares at James while clinching her knife. James and his silly crush. What an awful plan and even if it were to somehow work (which it won't) we're all going to die anyway. What's the point?

6

I'm sitting in the living room looking at a fashion magazine when Kim's phone rings. I answer in a tawdry voice. "Kardashian residence."

A booming voice that would startle almost anyone comes through the phone. "All right, you've had your fun. Your show is over. That was a nice little trick being able to fake cutting her toe off. Who put you up to this? Taylor Swift? Keanu Reeves?"

"Who the fuck is this?" I have no idea what's going on.

"I'm Lieutenant Waterman and I run this goddamn city!"

I laugh a little as I get up to look outside. I see a muscular man with a square face. He looks like Henry Rollins. In fact, when they make a film about me and my accomplishments here today Henry Rollins should play this guy. Who should play me? No one in Hollywood. No one is good enough to play me in Hollywood. Well, other than Daniel Day-Lewis, Christian Bale, and Tom Cruise. But they're not right to play me. It'd be too easy for them and I'm lacking too much pigment for them. So, it'll be a complete unknown you've never heard of. He'll have brilliant high cheekbones with low buccal fat that create amazing contours just like I have. Yes, that's exactly how it will be. So get your favorite shitty A-list Hollywood actor out of your head to play me because it's not going to happen. I'm the fucking Momentary Glamour Messiah and that just won't do. Anyway, I go on. "I'm sorry to tell you that you're not doing a very good job."

"You need to tell Taylor this isn't the way to handle this!"

"Seriously, what the hell are you talking about?"

"It's Keanu then, isn't it? I knew it was him. What the fuck does that maniac want?"

I finally realize this officer is a complete nutcase and decide to have fun with it. "He wants a series about Speed. Thirteen seasons of it and every episode is on the bus. That or Sweet November."

"What?! I can't fucking do that!

I do all that I can to hold back my laughter. "These are our demands. Oh and we need an ordained minister, too."

Waterman screams as loudly as he can. "Listen you Illuminati fucker…"

I hang up laughing. I can't believe what just happened. "Well, that was the police, I think."

"What did they want?" James asked.

"I'm not sure exactly." I say.

Suddenly, I realize the name Waterman is familiar. Why, though? It has something to do with the mother of these idiots Kris Kardashians. I can't remember exactly. But, that does remind me of a letter I wrote to Kris Kardashian. Yes, don't worry. You're going to be able to read it. Here it is!

Eric Ryder

Reality TV's Love Letters of Forgotten Flesh
In the Disgusting Vagina of Kris Jenner, United States of America: Endless
Fall of Rome
krisjennerturnedmeintoawoman@hatingmypenis.com

August 21, 2016

Kris Jenner
Kardashian Enterprises: Why Doesn't Anyone Notice Me? I'm Young
(stomps foot) Fuck! I Might as well be a Street Walking Prostitute
Lady of the Evening Ave. Trying to Find the Fountain of Youth with Penis
Forty Years Younger than my Vagina 20 Miles North of Semen from Affairs
Keep Me Young

Dear Kris,

Where do I begin? I have so many reasons to thank you, but it's hard
to pick a starting point. I guess I'll start with this. Marry me! I'm serious,
dear. I think it would greatly benefit us both. Think about it. I'm the
Momentary Glamour Messiah and you're the Undying Mother of Youth.
Can you imagine the baby we'd have? Holy fuck! Let's just hope she gets my
cheekbones since I don't need cinder blocks shoved in them to have the
sunken in cheek look. I'm sure we can find someone to make sure that it
happens, right? Anyway, when we have this beautiful child (with my high
cheekbones and low buccal fat) and your sociopathic nature she'll rule the
world. She'll be the Undying Glamour Messiah of Youth. With my fabulous
cheekbones and low buccal fat mixed with your money she'll look perfect
and never age her entire life. She'll own thirty homes that she doesn't need
just because she can. She'll have personal nannies who cater to her every
whim. Oh and of course she'll be so fucking interesting that she won't just
have her own show like your other daughters. No, she'll also have people
film the people who are filming her. She'll be so brilliant that people will
want to see the reactions of the cameramen who are filming her. It'll be the

second most popular show in this shithole of a country only behind her main show of course. What should we name her? Oh, fuck it we'll just name her the Undying Glamour Messiah of Youth. We'll call her Glam-Glam for short.

Okay, so we know our child Glam-Glam Rydashian will be amazing and rule the world. However, we forgot to touch on one subject. Mostly because it makes me cringe even having to think about it. But, how am I going to get my semen into your vagina? I guess I'll need a lot of WD-40. Ugh, even then is it even possible, dear? Call me crazy, but I don't find the cinder block cheek look too appealing. Wait! I have it, I really do. We can do the ultimate Hollywood couple cliché thing. We'll have a threesome because we hate each other so much and the intimacy we'd have to share in that moment would be too much. We need to make sure to keep it very superficial. No, you know what? We're having a foursome because we're going to reinvent the fucking Hollywood cliché. I get to pick the other women, though. One will be a hooker and the other will be a young woman who hates to be alone and just wants love. We'll talk the young woman into doing meth with us before our foursome and the hooker will of course bring her own living up to the awful hooker cliché. After we're fucked out of our minds because we're too stupid to enjoy the misery in life we'll have our foursome. Since I won't be aroused by you at all what we're going to do is very simple. I'll fuck the attractive confused girl without a condom and ejaculate into her vagina. After I do that the meth addict/hooker will come over and suck the semen out of her vagina. Then, of course she'll spit it out into your vagina while you're Tweeting and thinking of way to be a shittier person while making everyone else think they're the shitty ones. Well, Kris. There you have it, dear. There's my idea and I think you should consider it. Our daughter Glam-Glam Rydashian could change the world and just think we'd be the creators of her. Well, with a little help from a lost young woman and a meth addict. I really do hope you accept this once in a lifetime invitation. Now, if you'll excuse me I have to practice becoming bulimic.

Sincerely yours,

Eric Ryder

7

After a great deal of calling around and making threats and demand and being quite forceful, as only a man in my position can, I manage to round up someone to marry us.

Blah-blah, some Ordained Minister comes in to marry us. Elizabeth is pissed, James is pleased thinking his plan is working, Kim is oblivious, Khloe is hungry and craving vodka, and Kourtney tries to fight it some; so I place a knife to her cheek to make her say I do. There's an awful forced kiss that I make sure happens just to piss her off and let her know I'm in charge. Elizabeth is irate and screams at me. Blah-blah. Really a very poor plan by James and not even entertaining. I doubt anyone will pick one of his choices again and with good reason. So, don't worry the next choice will be given the proper attention it deserves. I just can't be bothered with this too much right now. Fade to black.

8

I step in front of the camera. I let the volatility of Hell's harbor sodden my tragedy in this berth of scorn. I can't help but glance at the Kardashians. I see Kourtney already knows it. The chapter is all but written. Boundless longing; nightmares for a girl in a fissure of deceit. Chalices all in a row filled with their claret breath. They'll be nameless like the faces in the forgotten pages. Scream now, do it. Let the lambasted climb into the silent echo of dusk's repose. My demur, forever trapped in the esoteric words that drip from the lips of this drowning saint; I drop to the bleeding silk. Smile, you're on camera. Bathe in the light of seditious bliss. It's time, it's time for the fucking show. You're made for this. You're the Momentary Glamour Messiah. Slit the throats of this mindless society now and bottle the screams for future generations.

I force the words out. I expect them to be languid, but to my surprise they're as fervent as the dismay that strangles the room. "Welcome back everyone. We have a big surprise for you."

Elizabeth is still bitter over what's just happened. "Do I get to cut Kourtney's lips off?"

I smile and continue. "Stick to the script dear. The surprise is as the viewer you have a chance to be swayed." I want Elizabeth to remember that while what we're doing is brutal we are not brutal. We are artists with a cause and if the cause creates a brutal nature, then so be it. But we are not brutal for the sake of brutality.

Elizabeth responds, annoyed and unenthusiastic. "What do you mean by swayed, Eric?"

"The lovely Kardashians will have the chance to state the reason they should be spared."

Elizabeth's tone improves a little. "Spared from what?"

I keep my Hollywood smile on and reply. "More effort, dear. Nothing too serious, really."

Elizabeth realizes I'm serious and despite her current anger for me she loves me and fixes the problem. She gives real effort. "What is it, Eric?"

I smile again, but a true smile this time. "I thought to myself what's the most useless part of the body?"

"Hmm, I don't know. I've never thought about it. But I do like that question." Elizabeth says with visible joy.

"Your little toe. So what happens if we cut it off?"

Elizabeth is so excited now that she can hardly contain herself. She screams lightly and claps. "Probably not a lot!"

I'm happy to see Elizabeth happy. Plus, the idea of one of the sisters losing a toe is also something that makes me happy. "Exactly, dear."

Elizabeth and I turn to the Kardashians and we both smile as we see the fear in Khloe and Kourtney's eyes. Kim is too vacuous to understand what's going on.

"Like who are you going to pick?" Khloe asks.

I ignore her question and continue. "So, girls. You're each going to have a chance to state your case. Personally, I don't think losing a toe is a big deal."

Kourtney, although scared, is still feisty. "Then like why don't you do it to yourself?"

I smile. "Tell you what Kourt. Since we're such a happy couple if you're chosen then I'll let Lizzie cut mine off, too." Luckily, for me Elizabeth doesn't hear what I've just said because she's too busy admiring her knives. She's wondering which one she's going to be able to use.

Kourtney glares at me.

I turn to James. "Put Kourtney and Eric, James."

James grins a little. "You've got it, Eric." I can see James is happy about this. He's so stupid that he thinks his little plan has worked.

"Okay, it's time for the begging." I say with my now famous Hollywood smile that the world can't get enough of.

9

Kourtney is sitting in front of the camera, preparing to elaborate as to why she shouldn't have her little toe cut off. Elizabeth is holding her knife, the one with Kourtney's name on it. She isn't too interested in what Kourtney has to say. The beauty of the blade is all she can see.

"This is like stupid."

If Kourtney's going to be so defiant I'm going to have to make sure she knows that I'm not playing a game. "Do it or instead of losing a toe I'll cut your tongue out now."

"I think, you, the viewer, should vote for me. I want to see Eric have his toe cut off too."

I'm vexed now. This stupid little bitch is trying to fuck up our moment. "Fucking bitch, do it right. State which one of your sisters should have it done."

She's still defiant. "No."

I know I have to make her my submissive little bitch. So, I walk in front of the camera and place the blade on her cheek. The blade finds its way into her mouth very gently. "Play the game correctly."

To my amazement she's still not realizing the severity of the situation. "I don't think that you have the guts to do it."

She's trying to embarrass me in front of the fucking world. This stupid little cunt bitch. "Turn the camera away for a moment, James."

James turns the camera away and I slap her as hard as I can. She lets out a cry and finally understands. "Do it you fucking idiot. Pick."

Kourtney glares at me, but answers. "It should be Khloe because she's stronger than Kim."

"No, which one do you dislike more?"

"I don't dislike either one. They're my sisters."

"Pick one and stop the absurdity or I will cut out your tongue and that's a promise."

"No, you won't." I stalk towards her. "Okay, I dislike Kim more," she says in a hurry. At last, at last, the show is finally starting to come along. "Why?"

"She's annoying, selfish, and just like a bitch and stuff."

"There's that "like" word again. I thought you were making intellectual progress, too."

Kourtney is upset and about to cry, but she forces herself not to. "Are you done?"

I smile at her and nod. "Yes, darling."

10

I sit back and watch Elizabeth prepare to question Khloe who sits in front of the camera. If Kim is the doll that comes with a removable fetus and talking action-figure husband who calls her bitch and instructs her when to be fashionably bulimic, then Khloe is the doll who comes with a psychiatrist who prescribes her seven different types of medication and diet pills just for fun. Oh, and of course you get her basketball-playing husband who comes with his very own brothel, filled with harlot dolls that all have a special suppressing gag reflex. If you're lucky and buy one of the first thousand the hookers come with meth. Also included, special edition biography documenting all the events in their lives that led to them to this point and how none of it is their fault. Abortion and suicide kit not included.

Khloe burps loudly before speaking. "Do you have any whiskey or vodka or like… whatever?"

Elizabeth taps into whatever motherly nature she has patience for. "No, Khloe. Not at the moment we don't. I need you to focus right now, okay?"

Khloe makes a face only fat people seem to be able to make. A strange look of having cement blocks stuffed in her cheeks and having an expression that makes it look like she's craving oatmeal with scabies and Balut with a side of ox penis. "I don't want to do this," she replies.

Elizabeth dons a mask of compassion. I have to admit she does it really well. She kneels next to Khloe and takes her hand. It's working. You can see the beast is softening. "Khloe, yes you do. You're the fat one, remember? How does that make you feel to be called the fat one by society?"

Khloe gives a minor fight, but it's clear she's going to break. "Stop, I have a hangover."

"Kim is the pretty one, Kourtney is the smart one, and you're the fat one who's a drunk. Do you want to be the fat one who's a drunk and missing her little toe, too?"

"Why are you doing this? Can I at least have some mouthwash or something? I can totally taste my throw up from last night." Her voice shakes, teetering on the edge of tears.

I glance at James, who mutters "gross" under his breath. I consider scolding him for talking when he shouldn't. I decide against it because Elizabeth seems to be getting somewhere. Best to keep the momentum going.

Khloe starts crying for real. "I threw up but didn't want to get it on my dress so I just held it in with my hand then swallowed it. But it tastes really bad."

Oh my. Oh my dear fucking God. This is too much even for these idiots.

Elizabeth squeezes Khloe's hand tighter to get her attention. But not too tight. Just tight enough to seem like a loving mother. "Khloe, darling, doesn't it bother you that you're called the fat one?"

Khloe screams in between sobs. "Shut the fuck up! Of course it bothers me, why do you think I'm a fucking alcoholic?"

"With every drink you have you're covering up just how hurt you are by your family. Especially Kim. She's the reason why society thinks you're the fat one."

Now Khloe's tears are completely out of control. "Even when I lost the weight they still called me the fat one. I worked out all the time and ate only fucking oatmeal with vodka in it for months and I'm still the fat one to the world. If I'm not the fat one then I'm the manly one who drinks."

I can't believe what a wonderful job Elizabeth is doing. Her patience is far superior to mine. Then again, I don't have patience for first world problems.

Elizabeth goes on. "I know, Khloe. It's simply not right. But you can change all of that now. You can be seen as who you really are. The strong one."

Khloe looks up at her. Her resemblance to a pig is stronger than it's ever been as she looks into Elizabeth's blue eyes. "How?"

Elizabeth smiles so kindly you'd think Khloe is actually someone she cares about. "By picking who deserves it most. Who really treated you poorly? More than anyone else?"

"Kim always did. 'Hey fatty, how many forties did you drink today?'"

Elizabeth pulls out her knives with the names of Khloe's two sisters on them. She shows them to her. "You don't have to say a name. You've gone through enough. You just have to point to a knife."

Khloe points to the knife with Kim's name/the Filth on it.

Elizabeth hugs Khloe. "You're so brave."

"Thank you. But, seriously, can I get some mouthwash? I swear I'm tasting puke, beer, and Taco Bell."

I stay back and it's a good thing because I wish I could kill her right now.

11

I stand in front of Kim as she sits on her bed. I examine her closely. I'm trying to tell if she understands what's going on at all. She constantly seems distracted. Almost like a child who loses their train of thought upon seeing a butterfly and then chases it for the next three hours. I'm half tempted to not say anything and see how long it'll take her to notice that I'm looking right at her. However, we're limited on time so I decide against it. The show must go on.

"Okay, Kim. Who's it going to be? Khloe or Kourtney?"

Kim looks up, surprised to see me there. "Uh, seriously?"

"Seriously."

Without any hesitation whatsoever, Kim says, "Kourtney. She's always been such a bitch to me. I made her career and she isn't even thankful for that."

I nod. "Why do you think that is?"

"She's jealous. She's always been jelly of me. I can't like blame her. But still she needs to get over it already."

"Totally," I say... the mockery failing to register with Kim.

Her face shifts a little. She's thinking, or trying to. She's upset and reminds me of a little girl whose gold fish just died. "When I came out with my doll line do you know what that bitch did?"

"No, I must have missed it."

"Okay, well, she like totally almost fucked me over. She waited until the last minute to sign so we could release her doll."

"What a bitch!" I say, and again the mockery is lost.

Kim is starting to get annoyed, gathering steam. "I know, it's like who wants a doll with only two of the sisters? We needed all three to make it work. The bitch had the nerve to almost not do it. I mean, little girls aren't going to want the dolls of just the pretty one and the lesbian truck driver looking Kardashian. They have to have to have the smart one, too. You know for the little girls who wear glasses and like read the books with words and stuff."

I try to look at her with something like the fake compassion Elizabeth showed to Khloe, but it's tough, given that I find the entire conversation hilarious. "How did that make you feel?"

"So angry, I like wanted to choke her and stuff."

The idea of Kim choking her sister to death makes me smile. I'd love to see her face turn blue and Kim take a selfie of it while it's going on. "Interesting. We'll save that for later."

"Um, like what?"

I smile and shake my head. "Nothing, you're all done here."

12

I walk towards the computer to see the results. Before I know it I'm smiling. James looks at me and smiles too. I walk over to the Kardashians who are sitting on the couch. Khloe and Kourtney are tied up, but I left Kim unbound. James goes to turn on the camera. Elizabeth is sitting down across from them, holding her knives.

The entire plan coming together in ways I had never imagined. "The results are in and the winner is Kim with eighty percent of the votes."

Kim claps. "OMG, I'm the most popular. But, duh. Everyone already knew that. Doesn't matter, still AH-MAZ-ING. Wait, did I do that right?"

Khloe looks at Kim in disgust. "No, Kim. You like lost. You're going to get your little toe cut off."

Kim looks at Khloe like she's stupid. "Uh, no I'm not."

Kourtney chimes in with a hint of fear in her voice. "Yes you are, Kim."

I walk towards Kourtney. "Sorry, darling. It looks like we're both keeping our little toes." Kourtney glares at me with the sort of disdain better suited to a couple after fifty years of marriage, marinating in the scent of fatality that suffused their rotting flesh.

Kim responds and explains to Kourtney why she's wrong. "This is a joke, Kourt. It's like a reality show with pranks. Nobody would want to hurt me. Hello, they were voting for who they like the most. The other 19 percent only voted for you guys 'cause they're jelly of me because they'll never be like me so they're like totally mad about it."

Khloe is enraged. "Idiot. They said eighty percent, Kim. That means twenty percent didn't vote for you."

Kim looks shocked. "Oh my God, do you know how ignorant you sound? You can never have one hundred percent of anything. That's like why they say ninety nine point nine something. If you could have one hundred percent of something we would have like one hundred percent the same DNA as chimps or whatever. We wouldn't be non-animals too."

Khloe's mouth is open in wonder. She turns to me. "Wow, I deserve a drink for having to listen to that, right?"

Even I have a hard time disagreeing with that, but we don't have the time. "Actually, yes. But not right now."

Kim soldiers on. "So like I was totally right wasn't I? Where are the prank cameras? I want to make sure they get my good side. Wait, what am I saying? I don't have a bad side."

I smile and take Kim's hand. "Actually, yes. You're right. You got us."

Elizabeth walks towards us and takes Kim's other hand. "Yes, it is, darling. You're so smart."

We lead her from the couch. "The main camera is over here," I say, showing her the wall of the living room.

Kim looks at it, but doesn't see anything. "Where?" She looks closer at the wall.

"Right here," I say before taking her by the back of her head and slamming her face first into the wall. Kim screams. I throw her on the floor and hold her down. She's in too much pain to fight back, or she's too stupid. Perhaps both.

Elizabeth grabs her foot and smiles. "Oh, such a smooth foot. I wonder if the blood will flow better on a foot this smooth."

I smile at Elizabeth. "There's only one way to find out, dear."

Kim speaks while crying and struggling, which makes it all the more enjoyable. "Like, you guys don't have to go this far to try and trick us with the prank."

Elizabeth takes a long, slow breath. She wonders aloud how the blood will stream and if it will fasten to her through the rest of this fray of misfortune. She takes the blade and with swift precision she cuts off Kim's little toe. Kim's scream pulsates through the furor of iniquity. Elizabeth smiles as the rapture of Kim's blood caresses her tongue.

13

In the aftermath, Kim is just a fucking delight, crying with her foot wrapped like a sandwich. Mainly because she insisted Khloe put a sandwich in it because she once heard sandwiches on wounds help with healing. Yeah… anyway, back to Kim being just a fucking delight. She should be smiling and happy, showering me with thanks for letting her staunch the bleeding. I suppose some people will never be grateful.

Khloe and Kourtney now realize that we're completely serious. Silver linings abound.

However, my joy is to be short lived. I see James handing Kim some pills. I walk towards him with madness and rapine choking my thoughts. "What the fuck do you think you're doing?"

James is confused. It isn't any wonder that his life has been a complete failure, other than meeting me. "What? They're just pills for the pain." He's so unsure. So insecure.

To say I'm amazed by the level of stupidity here would be an understatement. He seems to have forgotten what we're doing. "Idiot, she deserves pain. Look at this moron. She's the filth. The fucking filth. Do you not understand that?"

He's nervous. It's in his eyes. "I just thought…"

"Don't ever try and think again! You do what I say and *only* what I say."

James is too scared and embarrassed to realize just how much he'll hate me in a few minutes. Caught in this momentary lashing he clears his throat, lowers his head, and says, "Okay, I just…"

"No, you just fucking nothing. You're nothing. You think nothing. You only do what I say. Now pick up the camera and film."

James looks at the floor while walking to get the camera. I think he's probably imagining taking one of Elizabeth's knives and repeatedly stabbing me with it. I smirk at his thoughts. I know him too well. Why wouldn't I? I'm me and he's him. Smart and stupid. Insightful and insight-free. As I turn to face Elizabeth I subtly motion for her to go to James and console him. I want him to believe he actually has a chance with her. I want to see where it'll lead him. I already know what Elizabeth's reaction will be once he reveals his true feelings for her. Elizabeth is… a temperamental individual to say the least. However, her love for me is something that can't be questioned. I have to admit one thing. I find an imperishable dejection when I think about her love for me. I truly wish I could feel *something* for her. Maybe I do feel *something* for her based on the simple fact I wish I did. Perhaps it would be more accurate to say I wish I felt something stronger for her. Am I even capable of that? Am I forever stuck in this disunion with humanity? I remember at a very early age feeling like I had been dropped in from another universe sent here to observe these strange beings. It felt like it was my job to watch them closely and do my best to mimic them while I'm here to research them. I would know when someone felt something for me even then, but I had no idea how to feel it too. In the end anyone who gets too close sees me for the excavated caricaturist that I am. But the real question is: would I even want to escape this disunion with humanity? What would I be without it? I imagine I would be like every other defeated person on earth. In the end I don't want to lose it at all. I wouldn't mind having the ability to feel it in certain situations, though. At least for Elizabeth. Is my longing to even feel this my own mutilated form of love? The unadorned love that presents itself in starry visage of disentangled ardor. It is safe to say if there are soul mates Elizabeth was thoroughly fucked both vaginally and anally. It is also safe to say if there are soul mates I am my own soul mate making me equally fucked in a complete different way.

I gather myself as James picks up the camera. Elizabeth is laughing as she's sitting on the couch, hugging Kim. It's time for the Momentary Glamour Messiah to return. The burden of glory has such a weight to it. I smile and with that we're back on. "Welcome back to Killing the Kardashians. I'm sorry that you had to see and hear that. However, it was necessary."

To my surprise I hear Kourtney speak. "Why?"

What the fuck is this bitch doing? Does she not realize what's going on here? I turn to her and not hiding even a slight bit of vexation I open my mouth, which is nearly foaming. "What?"

Kourtney's droopy eyes almost look like they're about to shut and she's silently going to die and nobody would even notice. "Like, why was it necessary?"

"You're fatuous reality TV stars. You're famous for doing nothing. So, we're now famous for fucking with the idiots who are famous for nothing."

Kim looks up at me. Elizabeth is still hugging in her in an almost torturous way. She speaks while making the ugliest face. "You already cut my toe off. You don't need to call me fat too."

Khloe jumps in quickly. "Like, it doesn't mean that, Kim. I think it's a type of category or something for TV."

"We're known for lots of things," says Kourtney, incapable of simply sitting there without commentary. "We have a clothing line and so many other things."

"Your ridiculous clothing line is only a success because of your stupidity." I'm shouting and I'm frustrated that it's gotten such a rise out of me.

Khloe proudly says, "I'm famous for my store."

"No, you're famous for failed diet attempts and for your husband fucking other women on your birthday while you're left alone with cake and whiskey."

Khloe does everything she can to keep herself from crying. "Why did you bring that up? I forgot how much I want some whiskey."

I'm at a rare loss for words other than "morons."

Elizabeth stands and walks towards me, wrapping me in her arms. "Do you remember when Khloe was arrested and she was asked about it in interview? She cried and thought it was so terrible."

"Yes, the joy of first world problems. Not only first world, but a first world rich bitch. Oh the horror!"

Elizabeth laughs and screams in a shrill imitation of the sisters. "Oh my god! How terrible. The horror of it all!"

Disgust is coating my tongue like a small band of caterpillars. "So awful. Now are you done with your stupid fucking questions?"

It's clear that the idiots are finished for now. "Anyway, back to the topic at hand," I say, in control again. "We need to do more. However, I'm feeling generous right now. So, I'm going to let Kim sit this one out."

In a hushed voice Kourtney finds a new way to piss me off. "How kind of you."

I try to hide my annoyance and can tell I'm not succeeding. "Lizzie, dear. Please shut her up."

Elizabeth joyously skips in front of Kourtney and pulls out the appropriate knife. She slides it softly against Kourtney's cheek, slightly cutting it, a fine line of red surfacing within a second. Elizabeth smiles and then casually puts duct tape over Kourtney's mouth.

"Now, before I was so rudely interrupted," I say, "We're going to let all of you vote on something a little more fun. Lizzie B., you pick for Khloe."

Elizabeth kicks up her leg like she's the romantic interest in a classic love story. She smiles and replies. "I think that darling Khloe should have to eat and eat since everyone thinks she's the fat one. She has to eat until she vomits."

"Brilliant. We've all had to vomit hearing about her so-called problems."

Khloe looks sad. "I thought you liked me," she says to Elizabeth.

Elizabeth pats her softly. "I do like you! I just like watching you suffer more."

I forgot myself for a moment and say something inadvisable. "Now, I have something special for my wife."

Elizabeth picks up a glass on a nearby table and throws it across the room. "She's not your wife!"

I try to recover from my error. "Only legally. And I was joking."

Elizabeth shouts. "Do we follow the law? So, you won't follow this one."

I'm already tired of this fight. "Okay, you're right. You're the only one for me. Good enough? Now, it's time to move on. For Kourtney I pick she has to read an apology."

Elizabeth perks back up. "What sort of an apology?"

"An apology for endless puerility. However, this is where it's different. After the apology the audience will vote on if they feel it was heartfelt or not. If they vote yes, then nothing happens. However, if they vote no, then they'll vote on something else."

"What happens if Khloe wins?" says Elizabeth.

"Then Kourtney is off the hook for this one," I say.

Elizabeth smiles a little. "This is so exciting."

14

The phone rings. It's the police again. "What do you want now?" I ask, hoping I sound as annoyed as I feel.

The lunatic is screaming at the top of lungs. "You lying motherfucker! We talked to Keanu and he doesn't even know who you are."

It feels like I'm on another planet. "Oh, who would have thought that?"

"You'll be disappointed to know we let him go."

I laugh. "That's too bad."

Lieutenant Waterman is quiet for a moment. "Wait a minute," he says, "I know what you're doing. You and Keanu knew I would figure it out and I would end up having him arrested. But if you pointed us to him right away then it would seem so crazy and we would let him go after we question him! Then he's in the clear because we've ruled him out as a suspect. Oh, Keanu, you fucking clever psychopath."

And they'll say that *I'm* the crazy one. "Would you expect anything less from the man who was in Little Buddha?"

"I knew that was a subliminal movie to make people think the Illuminati isn't real!" It's like watching a dog swell up with pride because it successfully fetched the stick yet again.

Few things are as enjoyable as working a loon up into a lather. "The world will be rebuilt in Keanu's image. Now show Hardball on every channel. It's what Mr. Keanu wants."

"I will not help the Illuminati brainwash people even more than they have!"

I cover my mouth to hold in the laughter. I force myself to remember how much I hate the Kardashians and everything that they represent and the moment of levity evaporates. "Do it or I'll start cutting limbs off."

Waterman is screaming nonsense about the Illuminati for another ten seconds before he realizes I hung up.

I laugh as I walk back into the living room. James was listening while I was in the kitchen and is completely confused by my half of the conversation. No surprise there.

"What was that all about?" he says.

I shake my head. "Don't worry about it." Then I hear an annoying, whispering voice. It's Kim. She's waving me over to her. "I like have an idea and stuff."

I'm slightly interested, but also nauseated by the thought of Kim having an idea. "What is it, Kimberly?"

She's like a dog who's overly happy after their owner has returned from a long trip. "Oh my God, like I know I'm super popular but if you wanted money so much I would just give it to you. You don't need to sell my toe. Like how much is it worth, though? Like four hundred million?"

I just don't understand the world we're living in. It exhausts me. I mean, is all of this shit real? "No, it's only worth forty million. To get the full four hundred million I'll need your whole foot. Unless you can give me the rest of the cash."

"No, I think I'm like worth like seventy five million. But oh my god, fab idea. I could make a bunch of sex tapes if you get the guys in here. OMG! Even a fabber idea than before. I could make a lesbian sex tape with Caitlyn."

Khloe cries out in shock. "Kim!"

Kourtney joins in to fill us in with her always brilliant wisdom. "You can't do that Kim... he's like our dad or whatever."

Kim looks at her sisters like they're idiots. The irony is suffocating. "Uh, no. That was as Bruce. Now he's a she and she's Caitlyn and she was never married to our mom as Caitlyn so it's totally okay. OMG, such a great idea I had. I'll probably have enough left over to get a new closet of shoes, too. Who's the smart one now, Kourt?"

"That's disgusting." Khloe says.

Kim holds her head high. "You're just mad because if you made a sex tape it'd be in the Chris Farley section."

Khloe tries to break free from the ropes. "Fuck you, princess. Let's go right now. Untie me."

Kim casually looks away from Khloe and continues talking to me. "OMG, another idea came to me. When is uncle O.J. Getting out of prison? I could make one with him."

Elizabeth is examining Kim's blood on her knife. James runs over to me, completely ignoring them. "The results are in, Eric."

I shrug. "I'm a little disappointed to see this bickering end, but okay. James, turn the camera on."

James rushes to obey.

I quickly focus and notice how easy it's becoming. I really am a natural. "Welcome back to Killing the Kardashians. We're very excited because the results are in. Tell 'em, dear."

Elizabeth skips over happily. "Thank you, darling. The winner, or the loser in this case, is Kourtney."

I smile at Elizabeth and give her a nod of approval. She's elated.

Elizabeth then skips over to Kourtney and hands her a paper with an apology she wrote for her. "Compliments of Lizzie B."

Kourtney looks like she's about to vomit. "You can't be serious."

"Oh, but we're very serious dear." I hope she can tell how amused I am.

Kourtney looks at it and makes a face. "I'm not reading this."

I hold the knife up so Kourtney can see it clearly. "Want to rethink that?"

Kourtney hesitates a little. "Fine."

I smile. "That's my girl."

Elizabeth immediately starts to scream over what I've just said. "Hey! I'm your girl."

"I didn't mean it literally!" I've yelled more tonight than in the past year.

Kourtney shakes her head and reads it without any emotion. "I'm sorry that I'm such an ugly moron. I should also apologize for saying 'like' three hundred times in a minute."

"Read it like you mean it," I say. "I can tell if you're sincere, and sincere that was not."

Kourtney sighs and continues. "I would also like to apologize for my sisters and the fact we're all stupid whores."

A sudden fit of anger overcomes me. "Wait, stop filming! Stop!"

James turns the camera off.

I shake my head and glare at Elizabeth. "This apology is horrid. This is not how I told you to write it."

Elizabeth looks at me with all the innocence of a child. "I didn't really have a lot of time."

Ah, but I know exactly what she did. "Fucking hell, are you serious, Elizabeth? You just rushed through it so you could admire the blood on your knife."

Elizabeth makes the face that children make when they're caught doing something they shouldn't. "Welllllllllllll," she says.

"What the hell is wrong with you? If we don't do this right people will stop watching."

Elizabeth shouts. "I'm sorry! But the blood from Kim looked so different than the blood of kittens and rabbits. You wouldn't believe it. Like, really! It's like a magical bloody forest and when you think you've seen it all you come across a new part."

Kourtney whispers to herself, distress flooding her face. "Like, oh my god. We are so going to die."

I *can't* stop *yelling*. "I'm busy with the police and coming up with ideas and you can't do this one thing for me?"

Now Elizabeth is defensive. "She should just come up with an apology on her own anyway!"

I ponder the idea for a moment. "Actually, that's not a bad idea. Well done, Lizzie."

Elizabeth smiles and runs over to me. She kisses me forcefully. "Love ya, darling. Can I go back to my knives now?"

I'm focused on this new idea now. Totally zeroed in. I don't even want to think about anything else. "Sure. James, turn the camera on."

James turns the camera on.

I go back to the show. "We're sorry about that. However, I just had a superb idea. The speech wasn't working. It isn't fair to you the viewer nor was it fair to Kourtney...she should come up with her own apology."

Elizabeth continues to admire her knives, especially the bloody one. She doesn't even realize we're back on the air.

"So, Kourtney," I say, "please come over here. This is your moment."

Kourtney looks at me confused. "What should I say?"

I grab her and pull her close to me. "Say what comes from the heart!"

"Um, like, what if I'm not sorry?"

I smile and pull her even closer to me. "Well, you will be."

Kourtney takes a deep breath and knows she has to do it or I won't be happy. We've all seen the cost of my unhappiness. "Okay. I don't know what we've done or what I've done to cause people to hate me so much, but whatever it is I'm sorry for it."

I laugh in disgust. "All right, I know the viewers and I know what the results will be. So, we're just going to skip that part this time."

Elizabeth looks up at me. "Do I get to use one of my other knives?"

I calmly shake my head. "Not now, Lizzie."

Sadness creeps over Elizabeth's doll-like face. "Aw."

"As I was saying. I know our audience and I know they'd vote that was a pitiful apology. We need more effort and if we're not going to get it then I'll take over. So, here are your choices in the next vote for dear Kourtney. One: we shave her head. Two: We use an idea from earlier that wasn't picked. However, instead of Khloe just eating until she vomits from disgusting junk food, well, now Kourtney has to feed it to her."

Kourtney looks at me with a shudder. "You're a psychopath."

Her disgust for me gladdens my heart. "No, unfortunately I'm not. Now, time for the third option. We "fix" this stupid bitch so she can't have any more kids ever. We'll be saving our already mindless society from even more mindlessness."

Kourtney fights back. "Can we vote on which one of you is a bigger lunatic?"

Even I can see the humor in this. Her hate for us—and for me in particular—brings me an inexpressible joy.

15

While I'm in another room talking to the police on the phone. Elizabeth is left to watch the Kardashians. However, I took her knives away from her so she isn't tempted to use one.

Kourtney sees this as her chance to try and manipulate Elizabeth. "Why do you let him treat you that way?"

Elizabeth looks at Kourtney confused as she sits across from her. "Huh?"

Kourtney goes on. "He completely embarrassed you for the entire world to see."

Elizabeth is still confused and is starting to get annoyed because of it. "What are you talking about?"

Kourtney can feel the uneasiness of the situation and does her best to assuage it. "He married me and let the world see it. You're supposed to be his girlfriend."

Elizabeth yells. "Shut up! He only did it for the show."

Kourtney looks away for a moment before responding. "If you say so."

Elizabeth feels a wave of anger wash over her. "I might not have my knives but I can push your eyes into the back of your skull."

Kourtney realizes it's time to back off now. "Okay, okay."

16

Meanwhile, I'm on the phone with this fucking psychopath of a cop Waterman.

Waterman is screaming and it's hard for me to pick up exactly what it is he's saying. I manage to hear. "If you fix her I'll fucking fix your entire family alive or dead."

"Our demands haven't been met." I'm like a sculpture of tranquility itself.

"NO, NO, NO. You stupid shit. I called everyone and no one wants that fucking show back on. In fact, people want it erased from their memories, not brought back."

Waterman never disappoints. "Sorry, but those are the demands. I know it'll take a little while, so we can compromise."

"I won't compromise with the Illuminati."

"You will or you'll be sorry. Until you create Speed the series." I pull the phone away from my face and pretend I'm talking to someone. "What?" I say before talking to Waterman again. "Oh, he also wants you to show every Bill and Ted movie on national TV."

Waterman shows he's not only a lunatic but an idiot too. He seems like Hollywood's idea of what an officer should be with his retort. "He's in there?! How did he get in there?" Without allowing me to respond Waterman screams for back up to help with Keanu and then hangs up.

17

I walk back into the room and give James and Elizabeth the update. "They're begging for us not to "fix" her. Oh and they think we're the Illuminati."

Elizabeth smiles. James doesn't even seem aware of what I've said and walks to the computer to look at the results.

"The results are in, Eric." He talks like a man with purpose and power. He has neither.

Now I see why he ignored me. I don't much care of it, but it's at least understandable. I reply. "Great, turn the camera on James."

James turns the camera on and focuses in on me. I look brilliant as always and I'm ready to go. "Well, we're back and the results are in. So, Lizzie. Who's the winner?"

Elizabeth reads the results and is visibly excited. "The people picked to feed the fatty."

"Ah, I'm a little disappointed. Our viewers picked momentary hilarity over a lifetime of freedom from this strumpet's future offspring."

Elizabeth pats my arm. "Cheer up, Eric. It'll still be great. Maybe she'll choke and I'll have to cut some of the food out of her throat."

I hug Elizabeth. It's all about perspective. "You're right, Lizzie. Time to feed the bitch."

18

Khloe sits in front of a table full of chips and cookies in the kitchen. Kourtney sits beside her. Kim is watching a video she made of herself while she was taking selfies. She's also looking at one of her selfie books while watching the video. No one is watching her and why should we?

I motion for James to start filming and tap into my brilliant Hollywood persona. "We're back and it's time to feed the bitch. I hope you're as excited as we are. Well, you should be because you're the ones who picked this!"

Kourtney like she's about to cry. "I'm not doing this."

I put my hand on her shoulder and pretend like I have empathy for her in that moment. Then I quickly show her that I don't. She needs to remember right now she's my toy and I'll break her when I feel like it. Until then I don't mind removing a few limbs just to see what happens. "You continue to act like you're not going to do what I say. Yet, you know exactly what will happen if you don't."

Kourtney is obviously repulsed by me, but she keeps quiet.

Khloe looks up me and it's clear she's trying to get herself ready for this task. "Okay, psycho dude, I have a question. Can we change it to making me drink whiskey instead? I mean, duh, I love food but come on. Nothing beats whiskey. Besides, after I rinse with mouthwash in the mornings I take a drink of whiskey and you kind of interrupted that."

I smile and have good news for Khloe. "If you still want some whiskey after we'll let you have it."

"Okay, hurry up, Kourt. Feed me."

"I'm so sorry Khloe."

"Dude, I don't care! Just do it so I can have a fucking drink."

There is no intoxicant like power. Omniscience. Omnipotence. And an utter lack of mercy.

Kourtney begins to daintily feed Khloe cookies. Needless to say, this doesn't make me very happy. "No, not like that. Show them how it's done Lizzie."

Elizabeth picks up a handful of cookies and chips with Kourtney's hand and shoves them in Khloe's mouth.

I clap. "Well done, Elizabeth."

Kourtney makes a face like she's about to vomit as she feeds her sister. "This is horrible."

Ever the instructor, I have to correct the stupid bitch about what's horrible. "No, what's horrible is that three idiots have a TV show about nothing. What's even worse is that people actually watch it. Well, now they have something to watch."

Khloe begins to choke and Kourtney starts to freak out. "I'm done, I won't do more." Kourtney shouts.

"Oh yes you will," I say.

Kourtney shakes her head. "No, absolutely not."

Khloe yells with a mouth full of food. "Fucking feed me you stupid bitch! I need that fucking whiskey!"

Kourtney reluctantly begins to feed Khloe again. Kim finds her way to the kitchen to see what's going on. Soon after, Khloe can't take anymore and vomits. Elizabeth and I laugh and kiss. It's one of those things when you see your plan come full circle and you can't help but feel excited.

Khloe looks up at me with vomit dripping down her face. She somehow manages to find words in her uncomfortable state. "I feel horrible. I think I'm going to throw up again."

Kim is excited and claps as she looks at Khloe. "Oh my god, but you look so skinny. Throw up again, so you'll look even skinnier."

19

The Kardashians sit on the couch, dejected. Khloe is recovering and Kim is trying to look at her nails while she's tied up. She had to be tied up because she accidently tried to go outside after hearing a siren to see what it is. Kourtney watches me with pure hatred. I go back to reading a fashion magazine and feeling annoyed. Eventually I throw the magazine in the air and stand up because I'm fucking bored. What is this fucking bullshit? I mean, we have this stupid fucking country's reality darlings and nothing is happening. People should be sending me a crown made out of gold and bones from Nero. He of course didn't fiddle while Rome burned (the fiddle wasn't even created yet), but who cares? It's a great story. Caligula was too brutal even for my taste, though. He just wasn't very smart. He didn't play the game and because of it he was finally murdered and his body was consumed by dogs. When I die my body will be presented to the world. They'll have a tour of it and it'll be in a golden case. The commoners won't be able to touch me of course, but they should be allowed to see greatness at least once in their lives. Anyway, back to the commoners who think money gives them value.

I walk towards Khloe. "How you feeling, Khloe?"

Khloe isn't very well, as it happens, but she does her best to talk. "Uh, can I have some whiskey now?"

I smile kindly. "No, that offer has expired. You were supposed to ask right after."

Khloe lets out a scream. "Fuck! I need a drink, seriously."

I notice Kim motioning with her head for me to come talk to her. I put my hand up to Khloe to let her know we'll finish this conversation later.

Kim whispers to me, making sure her sisters don't hear. "Can we like make a deal or whatever?"

Excuse me?" I ask a little taken back.

"Like a deal and stuff, can we make one?" Kim asks eagerly.

I make an animated face to let the imbecile know I'm thinking about it. "I don't know. What did you have in mind?"

"Well, like, I totally have an idea. Super good one."

I nod. "Okay, what is it?"

"Like, you want money and stuff right? Like also to not go to like prison and stuff too, right?"

Reaching rapturous heights of sarcasm, I say, "Yes, that's exactly what I want."

Kim interprets this as the utmost sincerity. She continues on with the conversation, thinking I'm actually interested. "Well, like, this totally just occurred to me. I know how we can get you off."

I let out a faint gasp of laughter. "Okay, let's hear it, dear."

In the most serious manner I've ever seen Kim in she proudly says, "cancer."

Needless to say, I'm confused. I watch her for a few moments. Her eyes look as vacant as a heroin addict who has just been raped by Jeffrey Dahmer.

I raise an eyebrow. "Excuse me?"

Kim prepares herself for what I know is going to be a long speech. "Yeah, it's like bad and stuff. Like, we can say this was totally a publicity stunt just like my sex tape. Yeah, like we'll say I have cancer and stuff and like I hired you guys to do all this stuff as a like um, what's the word? Oh yeah, a like metamorphosis thing. You guys represent the cancer and stuff and like you cut my toe off to show that like even though I lost it I keep going on and stuff 'cause I'm going to beat it. Then like, I'll get one of those bald wig things and use it 'cause I'm totally not shaving my head for real. Bald heads are totally gross and stuff. But people won't know."

"Wow, I'm amazed." I say tiredly.

"I know, right? If we do this you're totally off the hook and plus I'll make all this money and then I can write a book and call it like "Even Cancer Loves Kim K." Besides, like when I was getting divorced I talked to this young girl who had cancer and she told me you find out who your friends are when you're going through it. I realized I was going through the same thing with my divorce. Also, I got divorced twice so I've actually survived cancer twice."

I just... fucking wow... I mean... ? I don't even know where to begin or what to say. There's no reason whatsoever after all of this is over that I shouldn't be able to walk out of here a free man. Christ, I should be viewed as fucking Winston Churchill and Mother Teresa combined for what I'm doing here. I should be canonized when I do eventually die, too. Saint

Eric goddamn cocksucking Christ Ryder. That's how I should be referred to after all of this.

I focus and breathe. "So, if you do this you're going to give me money you make from all of this?"

Kim thinks for a moment. "Oh, I had a better idea for that 'cause I know you won't trust me. So you can have some like... Oh what's that word? It's a Tom Cruise movie name but I can't think of it. I can't remember, so we'll just call it Tom Cruise. So like, I'll give you some Tom Cruise to prove to you I'm keeping my word. Like, you can have nine of my ten Bentleys."

This one I actually have to laugh at. Hey, I like Tom Cruise. All I can say is watch Magnolia.

"Well, wait, they match my wardrobe. Hmm, what can I give you as Tom Cruise? Oh, like I totally know! You can have my daughter and stuff until then. I mean, she came from my body and stuff so she has to be worth like over the hundred billion at least. So like, until my cancer book makes enough you can just use her as the Tom Cruise. But like if I get pregnant during the time I have someone write the book for me you can just keep her and sell her. I mean, I can just keep making new ones and stuff. I mean, hello, I am Kim K. But I'll totally pay Khloe to have the kid for me this time because the added weight won't hurt her."

Kim obviously stopped whispering long ago. Privacy abandoned, Khloe decides to join the conversation. "Uh, Kim. You already have another kid."

Kim is confused... again. "Wait, what? Is it a boy or a girl?"

Khloe looks shocked. "OMG, he's your son! So like a boy and stuff. Don't you remember giving birth to him?"

Kim thinks long and hard for a moment. Then looks back at Khloe and asks a superb question. "Um, I think I might have hired someone else to carry him for me. Was it you?"

"No, I was there when you gave birth to him!"

Kim has to think again. The effort looks excruciating. "Oh, I must have been taking selfies and didn't notice."

Kourtney is annoyed. "Yeah you were and like you were really mad and stuff because he doesn't look like you or something. You wouldn't even take a selfie with him."

Kim puts her lips together forcefully. "I kind of remember that. Is my first, second, or third husband the father?"

Kourtney rolls her eyes. "Duh, you had him after your daughter."

Kim is annoyed now. "Uh, that so doesn't answer my question, duh!"

James walks up next to me. What does one say amongst people like these? I finally smile and say, "amazing, isn't it?"

James nods. "Wow…"

20

A little later, James is checking the computer as I wait anxiously.

James looks up at me. "We have just over 5 million viewers. The news channels have picked it up, too."

What the fuck! We're torturing these fucking idiots and people can't be bothered to turn off bullshit like American Idol now called America's Got Chlamydia or CSI Rhode Island or whatever the fuck it is they're doing now. "Ugh, it should be more. Oh well, turn the camera on."

He does.

The persona is coming to me so naturally now that I'm not even sure it's a persona. We are, to some extent, who we pretend to be. "The one and only Eric Ryder here. I've just been informed we have over five million viewers. So, while we're not where I'd like to be we are getting there."

Elizabeth happily jumps into the shot. "Be sure to tell your friends about us."

I grin at her. "Thank you, Lizzie. However, I must take this time to apologize for my outburst during the last vote. That won't happen this time. But, the choices will be a lot more violent this time."

Elizabeth squeals. "Which knife do I get to use, darling?"

I gently grab her by the shoulders. "Elizabeth, settle down. There will be plenty of time for that later."

Elizabeth looks at her knives and frowns. You can hear the sadness in her voice. "Kim's name is coming off the blade. Do any of you have a bedazzler?"

Kim's eyes light up. "Shut up! You like them too? When I bought mine Khloe and Kourtney told me it was stupid."

Khloe looks amazed as she looks at Kim. "Kim, hello, she wants to put your name on it to stab you and stuff."

Kim shakes her head in disgust at Khloe. "Nobody would use a bedazzler for that. They're too fun. It's in the closet over there. OMG, my Lite-Brite is in there, too. Kayne had a special one made of my face, so fab."

Elizabeth smiles at Kim, then goes to get the bedazzler.

It's all becoming so irritating. Maybe we've just been here for too long. Even Elizabeth is starting to get on my nerves. Guy born in modern day Israel whose identity was forged with the Roman God Mithras... please help me. I mean Jesus Christ… of course. Okay, calm down. It's fine. They're idiots, Elizabeth has always been… whatever it is that she is, and you're Eric goddamn Ryder. I quickly smile and I'm back, the consummate pro. "James, pick what happens to Kourtney and make it violent."

James ponders this for a moment, brow furrowed. "Okay. Since she acts like she's been dropped on her head as a child I thought of something."

"Do tell."

"We have her run full speed into a wall head first."

This idea is completely pathetic. But James is like the little brother you have to praise, always telling him he's doing a great job. Still, I can't act like it's brilliant because it's not. I find a compromise. "Hmm, not exactly removing body parts but I like it. It's creative. I didn't know you had that in you, James."

James smiles at me. "Thanks!" He looks conflicted. He's surely now questioning if he should still go ahead with his plan to try and steal Elizabeth from me. Sad boy. The only certainty is that it's all going to go horribly wrong for him.

I gather myself and look at Elizabeth. "Lizzie dear, pick for Kim."

Elizabeth jumps up and down. "Oh my, let me see here. Since she's already lost her little toe it's kind of tough."

She's painfully cute when she's thinking about mutilating people. "Use your creativity here."

Elizabeth shouts as loudly as she can. "I know. FFF!"

"Bloody fuck, what is that? Now you're sounding like them," I say.

"No! Five finger fillet! Hand down on a table with their fingers apart and I try not to stab the fingers."

Good. Good good good. Fucking insane people. I'm surrounded by them. "Brilliant!" I shout, which pleases her to no end.

Elizabeth drops to her knees and starts to pray. I can't tell if she's serious, joking, or a little of both. "Please let me win."

"Okay, the pressure is on now," I say. "For Khloe… Boy, this is tough."

Elizabeth kisses me on the cheek. "Isn't it? I know, pick something with a knife."

This woman and her blades. "Enough with the knives," I say.

"Sorry! They're just so pretty."

An idea begins to surface. "The fatty can probably pack a punch, no?"

Elizabeth puts her finger to her lips as she thinks. "Hmmm. I'm excited by that question."

"You should be dear. We bring in a professional boxer/fighter or whatever. A female of course. We have the fatty fight her until she can't fight anymore."

Elizabeth claps. "God, I love it. I hope there's tons of blood." She jumps on me and kisses me with rapid-fire smacking noises.

I catch Kourtney out of the corner of my eye. She looks at us with more venom than ever. "God, you two are freaks. Besides, a professional boxer won't agree to that, idiot."

I release Elizabeth and walks towards Kourtney, grinning. "If a boxer doesn't agree, then one of you loses your tongue on the air! But, it still has to win. You're skipping steps, darling."

"How long will this last?" Kourtney asks.

Elizabeth flashes the knife with Kourtney's name on it. "Until you meet the blood quota."

21

The Kardashians sit on the couch awaiting the results. I can't wait to see how we're going to hurt these disgusting fucks next.

Elizabeth shouts, disturbing my thoughts. "The time is up, Eric."

I get up and prepare for the show. "Camera, James."

James turns on the camera.

"Welcome back to Killing the Kardashians, live from the Hyacinth House. I'm Eric Ryder. Your slightly deranged host."

Elizabeth smiles. "I'm the completely sane and rational co-host."

Oh lovely Elizabeth. "That you are, dear. The results are in. I'm very excited about this. I hope you stupid fuckers voted for mine this time."

James reads the results from the computer and smiles at me. "You're in luck, Eric. Your pick is the winner."

An exaggerated frown creeps onto Elizabeth's face. "Aw, no five finger fillet."

I ignore her. "In the words of the Kardashians, that is cool with a K."

Kourtney responds. "We never said that?"

"Actually, Kourt," says Kim, "that's my saying. I totally sent a thing signed by like four hundred trillion people to the word book people to have cool spelled with a k. The K obviously stands for Kim."

"Shut up," I say, with more patience than they deserve.

Kourtney tells me in a bitter tone about the situation. "You're not going to find anyone willing to come in here and fight her, idiot."

She's calling *me* an idiot? I grab her and pull her in front of the camera. "If someone doesn't agree to box this bitch's sister she loses her only tongue. You have an hour. Well, traffic could play a part, so two hours. To show I'm serious." I take Kourtney to the wall and slam her head into it face first. When she falls, her nose is bloody.

James and Elizabeth cackle.

I'm feeling great again. I even feel like being nice to James. "James, you've done such a wonderful job I decided to give you a little of your pick."

James is elated. "Hey, thanks."

"What are friends for?" I say with a bow.

22

I'm back on the phone with Waterman. The phone won't stop ringing. Apparently I won't stop answering. He's screaming about something, which is his way. I haven't really been paying attention, which is mine. I suppose I should do that now. I get back into the conversation. "You just get her here if you don't want to have these bitches tortured on your watch."

Waterman just screams louder after hearing this. "I haven't worked on the force for over twenty years to take shit from a little punk like you."

"Listen, Waterman. Do you want to go down as the awful cop who not only let these girls die but who allowed them to be tortured too?"

"It's lieutenant Waterman you little fucking prick. I don't care if you kill everyone in that fucking house, you will show me respect."

"Okay, Waterman. I'm going to..."

Lieutenant Waterman grabs his megaphone and cuts me off midsentence. "It's Lieutenant Waterman! You stupid little shit, Lieutenant Waterman!"

I drop the phone over how loud Waterman is. "Motherfucker!" I shout.

I pick up the phone while Waterman is still screaming through the megaphone. I hold the phone away from my ear and shout. "Just get here fucking fast."

Waterman is still really focused on this. "Call me it!"

I agree knowing that if I don't we'll never get anywhere. "Fine! Lieutenant Waterman get her here fast!"

I hang up the phone. "Fucking lunatic."

23

The phone rings and I answer it. "She better be here," I say immediately.

Waterman picks up right where he left off with his intensity. "If you do you anything to this girl I will personally cut your skin off and wear it as a ribbon."

I have no idea the hell that means. "What the fuck?"

Waterman doesn't seem to care if I'm confused. He's more interested in screaming more. "You will not touch this girl."

"Christ, why would I? She isn't a fucking Kardashian."

"I would even fuck the old plastic mother of the sisters you have in there to ensure this girl is not harmed."

I'm amazed by this. "Wait, seriously?"

"What did I just say?!"

I laugh a little. "Yeah, but... isn't there a limit?"

Waterman stops and thinks for a minute. "I'd make sure she has to sign a gag order to never mention it to anyone. Especially her husband or my wife I mean."

I don't think Waterman sees the parallel, but that's okay because it's still amusing. I let him know I appreciate that. "At least you have some pride. Anyway, send her in and we won't harm her. You have my word."

I hang up and tell Elizabeth to get the door.

Khloe is visibly frightened by what's about to happen. "No, please no. I can't do this, seriously."

"Dear, you can handle this. You're more of a man than any of us. You could take us out with one punch."

Khloe starts to cry a little. "I can't fight a professional fighter."

I lean down next to her. "I believe in you. I know that you can do this."

Khloe continues to beg. "I'll do anything you want. I'll sleep with you."

I'm astonished and horrified and I hope my face shows it. "You have to be kidding me. I find all of you to be disgusting. I wouldn't sleep with any of you for any reason."

Elizabeth walks back in the room with a very large blonde woman. Elizabeth heard what Khloe said. She grabs a knife and runs at Khloe. I catch her and hold her back. I try to calm her down because we don't need to deal with this right now.

Elizabeth is screaming and trying to break free. "Stupid bitch!"

I continued to try and calm her down. "There will be plenty of time for that later. But we have to stick to the rules for now."

Elizabeth pouts while still trying to break free from me. "I don't wanna!"

I whisper in her ear. "It's just for now. I promise you're going to have your time with her. Don't worry."

Elizabeth finally calms down some. I slowly release her, keeping my with my hands on her just in case she gets out of line. She's still pouting. "You promise."

I smile lightly at her. "Would I ever lie to you, dear?"

Elizabeth responds. "Never."

I kiss Elizabeth like we're a normal couple.

Kourtney interrupts the moment. "Oh my God, you freaks. Can we move this along?"

Elizabeth glares at Kourtney before walking towards our guest. "Fine, this is Ronda."

Ronda looks at us with apprehension. Despite the fact she could literally knock me out in one punch we do have guns. So, I smile and walk over to her. I do my best to be polite. "Thank you for coming. It's very much appreciated."

She nods. "Sure."

I shout for James. "James, camera."

James turns on the camera while I stand in front of it and pull Ronda in front of it, too. "Welcome back. I'm Eric Ryder and this is Ronda... what's your last name?"

She looks at me like I'm joking. "Seriously?"

"I don't watch boxing or whatever." I explain.

"I only brought the gloves because... never mind. I'm not a boxer. I'm a mixed martial artist. I do a little bit of everything. And my last name is..."

"I'm sure you can hit hard enough," I say cutting her off. "This is Ronda and she's going to beat up the Pig for us." I look at Ronda one last time and laugh a little. This Khloe bitch is fucking done and I love it.

Elizabeth pulls Khloe from the couch and makes her stand in front of Ronda.

I explain how it's going to work. "If you take it easy on her there will be a lot of trouble for all three sisters. So, don't hold back."

Ronda nods. "Okay…"

Khloe's obsession with alcohol seems to never stop. "Can I at least have a drink of vodka or whiskey?"

"If you win this fight you can. You can have the entire bottle. Oh and unlike the last offer, this one doesn't have an expiration date. Also, I'll be your manager."

Khloe looks at me with hope. "Really, the entire bottle? What do I do?"

Elizabeth hands Khloe a pair of boxing gloves Ronda brought.

"Listen, champ," I tell Khloe, "You have to watch for her right hook. Wait, or is it left? Just duck and punch her and you got this. You're more of a man than all of your cheating ex boyfriends combined. Hell, throw a side of Bruce in there too."

I push Khloe in front of Ronda. She tries to focus so she can have a drink. "Yeah, like sorry. But I'm totally going to have to kick your ass for that bottle of whiskey."

Ronda laughs a little.

"Make the first move, Khloe!" I shout.

Khloe punches and Ronda ducks and hits her. This one punch knocked her senseless and that's that. Shit.

I advance on Ronda, still holding a gun just in case she decides she wants to kick my ass. "Okay, I did say don't hold back so that's a little my fault," I say, keeping my distance. "Tell you what people! We're not done yet." I grab Kim, who's limping, but not really in pain because I think she's actually forgotten that her little toe was cut off. "Ronda, this time, toy with her a little before you knock her out."

"This wasn't part of the vote," says Kourtney.

I glare at her. "Doesn't matter, we're improvising."

Ronda puts her gloves up ready to fight. Elizabeth is forcing Kim to lace up the gloves. I playfully put my hands up, acting like I'm about to box.

"Ew, these mittens are totally gross," says Kim, wrinkling her nose at the gloves. "Do I seriously have to wear them? I have a pair of Prada upstairs and stuff."

I laugh and shout. "Bloody her nose a little!"

Elizabeth joins in with me. "Give her a nice left hook or something."

A nice left hook.

Ronda gives Kim a left hook. Kim crashes the floor, despite having been hit with only about half of Ronda's power.

"Get up!" I yell at Kim. "Ronda, I told you to toy with her first!"

"I'm sorry, I tried, but..."

Elizabeth cuts off Ronda. "Hey, shouldn't your soon to be ex-wife have a turn?"

I think about it for a minute. "What the hell. I think you're right."

I grab Kourtney and push her in front of Ronda, who immediately punches her. She's out cold in an instant.

"Fuck!" I say, laughing. "Do you have to be so fucking strong?"

Ronda shrugs as we're standing among the waste of Kardashians. Then she takes her leave and exits the house. I can't bring myself to stop her. She played her part and I'll be damned if she's going to sucker punch me while I'm in the middle of my biggest scenes.

24

Time passes. Soon, inevitably, inexorably, I'm on the phone with Waterman. He's doing his usual shouting. "Did you get them all killed you stupid little shit?"

"Do you think we would allow them to die yet?"

"Who's we?" says Waterman.

"Who do you think it is?"

Waterman. Paranoid Waterman, what an exhausting way to live. "They're surrounding us, aren't they?"

I reply very calmly. "What do you think, Lieutenant Waterman?" With strong emphasis on Lieutenant. People put far too much stock in titles, as if the words are what make them what they are.

Waterman goes crazy and starts screaming at the other police to take cover because "they're" here and surrounding them. Now taking cover Waterman goes back to the phone. "What do you want? What does Keanu want?"

"Many things, is Speed the TV show on yet?" I can hardly finish the sentence before covering my mouth to laugh at this fucking idiocy.

Waterman screams even louder than usual. "I told you! Nobody would do it!"

"Fine, then we'll settle for a TV series of Point Break."

"What the fuck! Nobody is going to do this!"

Waterman is still screaming at the top of his lungs just before I hang up.

25

I stand over the Kardashians, who are still out. I place my finger over my lips as the camera is rolling. *Shhhh.* Then I yell as loudly as I can. "Wake-up you fucking sluts!"

The Kardashians wake slowly as Elizabeth and I laugh. I turn back to the camera. "As you can see, our lovely Kardashians are a little out of it. I think we should give them a break."

Elizabeth kisses me passionately. I let her go smoothly so she doesn't know how tedious these constant bursts of affection are getting. "What do you have mind, daaaaaarling?"she says.

"Well, I remember one amazingly horrible episode where Kim wanted to be a model. However, she's too short."

"Are we about to make her dream come true?!"

Yes, Lizzie! So, to our lovely audience I'm sorry, but there won't be anything to vote for this time. It'll be a bloody fashion show. "

Elizabeth is so excited she can't stop moving. "They are pretty bloody."

"Isn't it swell?"

"Here, let me help a little more." Elizabeth slashes Khloe in the face, drawing a new, insistent trickle of blood.

I grab her hand gently. "Now, now, Elizabeth," I say, taking the knife away.

"I just wanted to hurt her a little," she says pouting.

"They've gone through enough... for now. We'll be back with the bloody fashion show soon." I smile and everything fades to black.

26

Time passes, as time unfortunately must.

Now the Kardashians are dressed in their most lavish gowns. Elizabeth is holding up Khloe, who can barely stand.

I stand before the camera. "Welcome back, I'm Eric Ryder. You're in for such a treat. It's time for the bloody fashion show. Who's our first model, Elizabeth?"

Elizabeth pushes Khloe forward.

"Well, it looks like we have Khloe first. She's wearing a lovely gown designed by some douche from New York or Italy."

Khloe is dazed. "Where's my whiskey?"

I jump forward towards Khloe. "You look just lovely dear. You really do." I punch her in the stomach and she falls to the floor. "Who's next?"

Elizabeth pushes Kim forward who is crying and limping.

"Here we have the amazingly vapid Kim and she's wearing a gown from Finland". J   "Finland? Is that in Scotland or something?" Kim says as if she is trying to win a gold medal for being insipid and obnoxious.

"It's right out of Helsinki." I say.

"They have sinks in Hell?" says Kim.

Elizabeth pushes her into the wall. Kim falls to the floor moaning in pain.

"Last and certainly least is my horrible wife," I say. "My soon to be ex-wife."

Elizabeth pushes Kourtney forward. "We see my darling Kourtney wearing a gown from what looks like a drag queen's closet. We'll say from Idaho." This emcee gig suits me fine.

Kourtney turns red. "This gown costs more than your home."

I walk towards Kourtney and rip the gown. "Not anymore," I say.

"You fucking whore!" Kourtney is screaming, the whites of her eyes blazing out of her dull face.

I swell with pride. "Oh my! I thought we beat the stupidity out of her, but I think it's just in there too deep! Here, why don't we try this?" I spit in her face. "Maybe you'll respond to humiliation more."

Kourtney wipes the spit from her face and starts to cry. "Bastard!"

"Oh what the hell," I say. I push Kourtney to Elizabeth who then pushes her back to me. This goes on for a little bit while the two of us get our kicks.

Khloe starts to regain her composure. She stands up and sees what's going on. "Like oh my God. What's wrong with you guys?"

I stop and move while Kourtney is being pushed towards me. She hits the wall and falls to the floor. I go to Khloe and pull her up by her hair. I look at the stupid cunt with a hatred so profound that it is almost beautiful. "Perhaps we're drunk on your stupidity. However, I've never had a professional opinion. What do you think is wrong with me?"

Elizabeth happily answers. "I think you're a psychopath and I love it!"

"I was thinking more of a self-aware narcissist." I say with a shrug.

"You're fucking insane!" Kourtney's shrieks are probably sending every dog in the zip code into shock.

I couldn't have hoped for a better reaction. Stealing a page from Elizabeth's script, I skip towards Kourtney, who is still on the floor. I pull her up by the hair again. "One last blow for the show," I say before punching her in the nose. Blood streams down her face. It's perfect.

27

I smile with the camera on me. "Ladies and idiots we have the biggest news in the history of Killing the Kardashians. We're going to have a special guest."

Elizabeth claps and mocks the Kardashians. "Like, oh my god, who is it?"

"Kanye West, Kim's husband!"

Elizabeth waves two knives in the air like she's practicing semaphore. "Oh my God, I'm shaking with joy."

"Me too," I say, despite remaining motionless and feeling tired.

Eric and Elizabeth jump up and down, slapping each other almost exactly the way the Kardashians do. Soon after a Skype call rings from the computer.

Elizabeth looks at me with wide eyes. "I wonder who it is?"

"Why don't we find out?"

I answer the call. Kanye West is on the screen. He immediately starts screaming. "If you do anything else to my wife I'll murder you and your entire family."

Ah, the good old hollow, impotent threat. "Someone thinks they're in charge when they're not. Do you want to try again?"

Kanye screams again. "You motherfucker, I'm serious."

I walk towards Kim. I pull out a knife and place it on her cheek.

Kanye assesses the situation and manages to act properly for a moment. "Okay, okay."

I grin as the nitwit backs down. "That's better. Now, we're going to play a little game. It's called the act of love. It's simple, really. We'll start out with a few easy questions for you."

This is obviously too much for Kanye to comprehend. "Man, what the fuck?"

"Are you ready, Kanye?"

"Motherfucker I don't even know what you're talking about."

"That's okay," I say. "I won't hold it against you. First question. When did you first know you were in love with Kim?"

"Say what?" says Kanye.

I repeat the question in a different form so the lout will understand me. "When did you first know you wanted to spend the rest of your life with Kim?"

Motherfucker, I don't know. I don't care about no fucking history." Understanding. It's not easy to come by in these circles.

Now I'm confused. "History?"

Kanye responds in the most insipid manner. "Yeah, motherfucker. Everything I do is being written in history books and shit see. But, I don't read that shit 'cause I'm too busy writing history."

"I kind of doubt you can even read."

He's angry now. "I can read motherfucker. I just don't need to read about some short dude named Napoleon and shit 'cause I could conquer shit way better than he could."

"Actually, I can tell you don't read at all. Especially since Napoleon was actually almost 5'7". He's listed at 5'2" in French units. However when converted he was almost 5'7". A little above average height for his time."

Kanye screams so loudly that lines appear on the screen. "Motherfucker this ain't no fucking history class and shit. I just know I be conquering shit better than him. Did that motherfucker have a loft in NYC? That motherfucker get to meet Obama and shit like me?"

"Wow, okay. Touché, you got me there." I never get sick of hearing myself laugh.

"That's right, motherfucker. I'm a fucking genius, that's why. I don't even read and shit and I'm still a genius. Look at you. I'm a non-reader and shit and I'm proud of that. I don't need no book's autograph and shit, but you be a reading dumb fuck."

I suppose this is what happens when you're married to a Kardashian. I doubt he was very bright to begin with or he wouldn't have married one, anyway. Still, this is a new level of stupidity. "That statement would even make Diogenes think."

Kanye seems angrier now, but who really knows. The man's resting state has never been one of tranquility. He goes off on some long tangent. "Yo, motherfucker I don't even know who or what that shit be. I care about my fucking gold, Beyonce, and defending O.J. and Chris Brown. I just gotta say this again 'cause it's been buggin' me and shit. Give Chris a break. Who ain't wanna slap their bitch around from time to time, you know? And O.J.

let's be real here, fool. He's amazing and shit what he did, is he not? What he did, when he did, what he did. Nobody can deny that shit, for real. Real ass motherfucker and people be hatin' and shit. You show a real OG like O.J. that kind of disrespect you be askin' for it."

I clap, applauding his brilliance. "Love it."

"Of course you be lovin' it. I said it, everyone be lovin' the shit I say. I'm the son of God, motherfucker. Nah, fuck that shit I am God. When I be prayin' I be prayin' to myself then I make my prayers come true 'cause it's what I do. I'm the ghetto Pope."

I find all of this to be very amusing, but I know I have to keep him on the subject at hand. "All of this great, but we're getting off track. Back to the question. When did you know you wanted to spend the rest of your life with Kim?"

"Yo, this is a stupid fucking question. I'll tell you the answer anyway, though. I saw this bitch and shit and I knew by that fine fat ass I wanted her. 'Cause I like them asses big and I knew it was the ass of a mixed race bitch. If it wasn't for race mixing there'd be no video girls. Me and most of our friends like mutts a lot. Yeah, in the hood they call 'em mutts."

How can one person contain so many laughs? At least one more, because there it went. "Well, if that isn't the best answer in the history of mankind I don't know what is."

Kanye is obviously proud of himself, like he just got a gold star made of real gold. "That's right, that's right, motherfucker. Yo, you ain't so bad. At least you got some sense and shit you see how awesome I be."

"I do. Next question. What's your favorite thing about Kim?

Kanye responds without thought, as if he's been waiting for this question his whole life. "Probably have to be when I told her I'm gonna make a book of all my tweets and call it tweet-book she thought it was dope."

Fucking cretins. "It does take a special woman to see the brilliance of that idea."

"Oh yeah, I thought of one other reason. Yo, check this, I ordered room service this one time and I knew these motherfuckers cut all my food with the same knife. I could taste it. Beef flavored pineapples. Well, my bitch didn't stand for that shit. She call 'em up and make them remake it in front of me and use seven different knives and shit. Didn't even need all seven, but it's nice to be prepared, ya know?"

I could do this all day. Maybe I *should* do this all day. But as great as this dumb fuck is, this is starting to take too long. I try to hurry this conversation along. "Superb reason. Next question. If Kim makes it out of this alive where do you see the two of you in ten years?"

"Oh, that's easy. Everyone knows I wrote my song Perfect Bitch about Kim. So, ten years from now I'll probably be working on Perfect Bitch part three or four by then."

How disappointing. Reboots and sequels. Creativity used to be a precious commodity. "I was hoping for more, really."

Kanye starts screaming again. "Motherfucker I ain't done and shit. Also, I see myself as the president and shit and Kim as the first bitch. You know it's like Obama, you be a good president and shit. You may be talented, but you're not Kanye West. I mean damn motherfucker...by fifty percent I'm more influential than Stanley Kubrick, Apostle Paul, Picasso... fucking Picasso and Escobar. By fifty per cent more influential than any other human being. Even Obama."

There we go, now I'm proud of him again. Amusing man. "Brilliant. So, one last question. Are you willing to take your wife's place here?"

Kanye is a little confused by this question, but it's hard to hold it against him. "You mean like become a fine ass woman and shit? Nah man, I can't do that. I mean, I could, but I'm not."

"No, are you willing to take her place as our hostage? If you do I promise not to harm her anymore and as soon as you're here she's allowed to go free. But, you have to stay and see how it turns out, which could end up with you dying."

Kim nods in excitement and claps. She turns to her sisters. Straight out of Mean Girls (I wish this stupid bitch looked like Rachael McAdams and not an alien with plastic stuck in her face) she says, "Yay, I'm free! Sorry bitches." *Snap snap.*

Kanye doesn't even hesitate with his response. "Man, you crazy? I mean, Kim is a fine bitch and all, but that ain't gonna happen. I'm Kanye West motherfucker. It'd be like the fall of Rome and shit if I died. You know, maybe for Beyonce I might do it, but not for Kim. Sorry, bitch. I love you, though. Oh yeah, one last thing, bitch. If you don't end up dying and shit we got dinner plans tomorrow in NYC with Chris Brown. He wants you to show his new bitch how to cover up bruises on her face and shit. Love you."

Elizabeth and I laugh hysterically while Kim gets slammed by this new tidal wave of dejection. "Sorry, Kim," I say. "It looks like you're stuck with us."

Kim is in shock. "I can't believe it. I thought he would do anything for me."

"I know, I thought it was true love." I say.

"I know... Oh and I'm totally prettier than Beyonce." And that right there was the summation of everything that was wrong with her. Signed, sealed, delivered, and derp.

Khloe and Kourtney glower at Kim. Fractures and fissures, everywhere I look. Kim doesn't even notice and already seems to be over the fact that Kanye wouldn't choose to save her. I'm almost jealous of how nothing sticks to her.

28

Elizabeth looks at the Kardashians, then to me. She's a little perturbed, but I'm not sure why. Hesitantly, she says, "Eric, I know this is fun and all, but when do I get to stab another one?"

Well, I could have guessed after all. I must need sleep. I give her the thumbs up. "Very well, I won't promise you get to stab someone again, yet. But, I'll give you that opportunity."

Elizabeth bounces in excitement and kisses me on the cheek. "Thanks, darling!"

I look at James. I can see the pain in his eyes as he just watched Elizabeth kiss me. He envies what I have and I envy what he feels (in some aspects, anyway). "Turn on the camera James."

James turns the camera on, the act taking on the feel of a ritual at this point.

"Welcome back to the most entertaining show on the web. The only reality show based on reality."

Khloe sniffs. "Our show is based on reality."

Ugh. Where to even begin with that one? But I decide to be the bigger person. Someone has to and we have things to do. "Sure it is. Anyway, we've been having a lot of fun. That's fine. However, we came here not just for fun. Society needs to understand why we're doing this."

Elizabeth giggles. "The neighbors ran out of kittens, too."

I deliver the options once more." "First choice for the vote. We recreate Kim's famous and disgusting photo that no one will ever forget. However, there will be a few painful surprises for this picture. Okay, James. Pick something."

James jumps in despite the fact he's supposed to be filming. "Who am I picking for?"

Should I jump down his throat for this or not? No focus. No confidence. James in a nutshell. However, I guess I should be proud of him because he's adapting to the situation. You take your progress where you can get it. "Your choice," I say."

He smiles at me. "Okay, Kourtney."

"Don't hold back," I say. "Let your mind run wild, anything you want."

James thinks for a moment. "Why don't we have the viewers send in…questions?. Questions about history or culture or whatever. For every question she gets wrong we hit her."

Elizabeth cheers. "Good one, James! It's funny because they're so stupid here." Elizabeth says pointing at her head. I'm not sure if she's mocking them… or… never mind.

"I love it, James." If I make him feel good now, everything later will feel even better. "Okay, Lizzie B., you're up. Pick for Khloe."

Elizabeth bites her lip while she thinks. "Anything?" Sometimes I think she wants to be Dolores Haze. Absently, I wonder if she has ever read *Lolita.* And if she wanted to be Dolores, what am I? As psychos go, I'm in good company with Humbert, so I take all of these hypotheticals as a compliment.

"Anything my dear."

Elizabeth claps as the idea comes to her. She can hardly wait for the words to flow from her lips, ejecting them like spent bullets instead. "We put her against a wall and we each get three throws with a knife. Whoever makes her scream the most wins. I know the spot to hit where they scream the most."

I just can't believe it. It's unreal. How did I even meet this woman? She's fucking demented. I'm not saying it's a bad thing, but Jesus Christ. There's a giddiness bubbling up in me and I have to squash it, dilute it stifle it if I'm going to stay focused. "I like it. Let's set up the interviews."

29

Khloe sits in front of the camera. Christ, she's a masculine one. I wonder at what point in your life as a man you decide it's a good idea to stick your penis in her vagina. Better than the noose? Doubtful. How much self-hate is needed to do that? If I were to ever get to that point of such endless despair I think I would walk into the bathroom and put a gun to my head and blow my brains out. I wonder how much of it do you actually see before you die? Is it a glimpse of beauty? Is it like seeing the woman of your dreams in a crowded street before she disappears into the crowd? A quiet beauty that causes you to question if it really existed at all, or was it merely your own sorrowful longing for that Hollywood moment your mind created?

A sharp and masculine voice cuts through me. A brassy baritone, this one. "Are you going to like ask me something?"

I disengage from my thoughts in order to tangle with Khloe the beast as if she were Grendel's mother. "Why should you be spared…and who should take your place?"

Khloe is upset and lets me know it. "I'm totally protesting you."

"Why?" You'd think that I'd get used to being second-guessed. You'd think wrong.

Uh oh. Now she really lets go, and it's here that I see that what I thought was truly pathetic was not. *This* is pathetic. Tears find their way from the eyes of this monstrosity. She sobs like a person who actually has real problems. "I've totally done everything you've asked of me and I still haven't been given a drink. I mean, like, seriously... can I have a shot at least?"

The rage is hot and immediate. "Oh dear fucking Christ. Are you fucking kidding me, fatty?"

"Oh my God," she moans through tears, "I can't help it that I was born with genetics that make me fat and stuff and alcoholism is totally a disease."

A new coldness takes over my lungs, warring with the angry heat in my head. "Yes, divorce is obviously worse than cancer and alcoholism is clearly at least as bad."

"Like I didn't say that, but it so isn't cool to make fun of someone for being bigger."

"Oh yes, I forgot we live in a time where we should accept people with awful genetics rather than let them die or just kill them."

Khloe seems frightened now. Finally. "Like seriously, did you see the episode of our show where I meet with a woman who studies the minds of killers? She's totally going to have your brain one day. You're a psycho."

The rage is trending some vague evisceration whose edges I can't quite see yet. "Do you know what the greatest paradox is? By coddling the fat, the alcoholics, and the weak, rather than just ridding of them, we're not bettering them or ourselves. We're allowing their weak genetics to pass on so it can happen again and again. If we just slit your throats it would stop there. But, no, we allow your genetics to be passed on while the stronger individuals have to repress theirs for the sake of empathy. By doing this we're allowing your bad genes to flourish while the people with good genetics are forced to repress their nature. Before we know it we're living in a world of fat, dumb, and whorish cunts like you who have a TV show!"

"Like oh my God, seriously, look at your eyes and stuff. You're totally an Al Bundy type of guy." She's beyond my reach for the moment, which I can't have. In control there is everything.

Elizabeth walks over to me and pulls me aside. She whispers something to me. I don't have a clue what it is, but the softness of her voice is soothing. I walk back over to Khloe. I feel fine now. And what's this? The hint of a smile, returning once more.

"Okay, Khloe. Who do you pick?" I say in a completely different tone than a few seconds ago. I'm not feeling like myself. I wonder, not for the first time, if there's such a thing as a self at all.

"I told you already. I'm protesting. I'm not picking until I get a shot."

I'm feeling generous because of the sleepless Lethe of Elizabeth's abating breeze from a moment ago. "Will someone please get the lovely Khloe a shot?"

Khloe's excite-o-meter goes from zero to a zillion in nanoseconds. "Oh my God, thank you. I'd totally hug you if not for these ropes. Bring the bottle please."

James comes back with a shot of whiskey (and the bottle) and holds it for Khloe while she slugs it down.

"Okay, Khloe," I say, once balance has been restored to the universe. "You can have more but only after this. Who do you pick?"

Khloe responds without thought. "Kim."

"Why?" I ask gently.

"Like, I like the idea of you making fun of her stupid picture. I don't know what the big deal was, it was just stupid."

I smile. "You hate her don't you?"

Khloe thinks for a second. "If she wasn't my sister I would."

"That means you do." This will work better if she has no doubt.

Khloe thinks on it for a moment. "Maybe. I mean, like, when I was losing all my weight she was kind of a bitch about it.

"Do tell," I say.

"Like she would tell me I look so good but she was being sarcastic I could tell and she had this smile that was so..."

The poor thing is having a hard time so I decide to help her out. "Condescending?"

Khloe acts like she understands what the simple word means, but of course she doesn't. I wonder what it must be like to know *nothing*. "Um, yeah, that's it. Our mom also treats her like a goddess and her prized possession, too. So annoying."

I pat her knee. It's the size of a tree. "Thank you, Khloe."

Khloe pauses. "I have a question..."

Oh, what could it hurt? "Go on."

"Are you really going to kill us?"

I explain it once again. My throat is going hoarse from all of the repetition. "One of you will get to live."

"Which one?" She sounds so sad.

"That's up to the people. You'll have a chance to state your case, though."

Khloe looks like she's about to cry, then realizes she's an alcoholic and forgets about everything else. "Oh, can I just have the bottle, please?"

30

Kourtney's turn.

She sits in front of the camera. She's decided she's just going to get through this as quickly as possible. Resigned. Grimly resigned. She knows who and what I am now. Part of me wants to make her tell me everything she thinks she knows about me, but perhaps that can come later.

"It should be Kim." Kourtney says.

I raise an eye eyebrow, intrigued. "Why do you say that Kourtney?"

"I know we're all hated, but she's the main reason. We might not like be the smartest people but she makes us look sooooooo much dumber." It's hard to argue with her reasoning.

"Interesting," I say. "I'm glad to see you're playing the game properly now."

"Do I have a choice?"

"No, you don't." It's hard to keep the delight out of my voice. Most people will never know what it feels like to have complete control over someone. That's fine. More for me.

Kourtney trots out another exhibit, getting into the spirit now. "Also, she's like a terrible mother. I remember when she just had her daughter and she was crying all the time. I went in and found Kim taking selfies and I wondered why she wasn't taking care of her."

"And why wasn't she?" The key to always looking masterful is never to ask a question you don't already know the answer to.

"She said her hair looked perfect and she wanted to take a selfie to show everyone. She just had a kid to have a prize. I could tell she forgot she even had her in the room with her."

I smile with genuine pleasure. "You've been very helpful, Kourtney."

"I'm sure I have." Oh, she's so, so bitter, and it's so sweet.

31

Over to Kim, who now sits in front of the camera looking at her nails. She's not tied up because she's not a threat at all. What would it be like to actually have people see you as *harmless?* I can't think of anything I'd like less. I would actually welcome her to attempt to try and escape. It would be fun, I'm certain.

Kim looks at me like she's just finished eating rotted fish. "Which one of those bitches said me?"

I pace, turning my head as I move back and forth to keep my eyes on her. "Why do you ask that?"

"Oh my God. They both said me didn't they?"

She's smarter than I thought. Good for her. "How does that make you feel, Kim?"

"So annoyed. You know what. I pick both of them. They should both have to have it done."

I'm a little proud of her for trying to pick that. "I'm sorry, but that's not a choice, Kim. You can only pick one. But, I am liking your fire." It's a relief to have something about her to like.

"Well, can I think about it?" I braced for the wonderful litany to come.

"As long as you do so out-loud."

"Totally. So annoying. I could say Khloe because she's a fat skinny girl."

I smile. "What does that mean, dear?" Having low body fat I know what skinny fat means and it's something to avoid at all costs. However, I know that isn't what Kim is talking about.

Kim explains in the most perfect way ever, as only a Kardashian could. "Even though she's skinny now you can still tell she's meant to be fat. It's like all over her face."

Elizabeth and I both laugh our heads off. *Fatness as destiny. Wonder of wonders.* James smirks, but knows better than to laugh on the air.

Kim goes on. "Then you have Kourtney who is so jealous of me. She was so jealous when I married Kanye."

"Who wouldn't be jealous of you marrying a guy who's famous for interrupting artists better than him?" I mean Beck mostly. Beck is weird and artistic enough for me to respect. The other is still better than Kanye, though.

"I know, right? Wait, what?"

"Doesn't matter, go on."

"Ugh, so annoying," she says yet again. "I guess I have to go with Khloe for being fat for so long and still being fat like emotionally. Also, this one time when I paid for her Botox it cost like double because the doctor said he had to inject through all these extra layers because of her fat and stuff. So annoying."

Now I can't even pretend not to laugh. These dumb fucks make staying serious like Sisyphus pushing that rock up that hill in Hades. "You know, Kourtney said you're the dumb one in the group."

Kim gasps. "That bitch. If I'm so dumb then why did I make their careers? Did you know I'm the one who released my sex tape? Everyone thought it was a mistake, but I made millions and millions from it. It also made me even more famous."

"Clever, being famous for not being famous isn't that big of a deal anymore. It's good to fall back with the classic sex tape ploy."

Shots across the bow. Sarcasm remains undetected, Captain Eric. "Totally."

"It's been very pleasant, thank you."

Kim smiles at me. It me of a child's face if the child were missing half of their brain. "You know like when you're not being a total crazy person you're kind of nice. I like your eyes too."

I laugh a little. "Hang onto that thought." *Hang on for dear life.*

32

My turn again, in front of the camera. James has just told me great news. We've had a major increase in our viewers. Big time. Prime time. It works wonders for my mood and I have to inform the audience. "And we're back. We've had quite the jump in our viewers. We now have twenty-nine million."

James steps away from the computer with the camera on the tripod to announce the results. "The winner, with seventy-seven percent of the votes is your choice Eric. Kim."

"Oh my. It looks like we have to prepare. We'll need some supplies." There's a song in my heart that only I can hear.

I decide to make demands to the police. I leave the room while talking on the phone. While waiting, I can faintly hear Kourtney using this opportunity to talk to Elizabeth who's upset her choice didn't win. *Always the bridesmaid.*

"You totally know he's just using you, right?" says Kourtney. "I bet he isn't even letting anyone vote."

I peek back into the room. This is getting good.

Elizabeth glares at Kourtney. "Shut up."

Kourtney lowers her voice some to make sure I don't come back into the room. "I'm just saying like he's kind of an ass to you. I mean, like, he probably faked the votes so he could marry me."

The expression on Elizabeth's face is priceless. I'd a painting of it, actually. "He hates you! Ugh, you're so lucky he took my knives."

"Like, I don't like you either, but it's so obv he's using you. As women and stuff I do feel I kinda have to look out for you some. Even if you want to cut me up and stuff. He's going to take this too far. Do you want to spend the rest of your life in prison?"

Elizabeth sticks her shoulders back and stick her chin up. "We're not going to prison."

Kourtney is confused. "Um, like where do you think you're going after this is over?"

"We're going to kill ourselves." Elizabeth says this with a certainty born of madness.

Kourtney laughs and the sound is condescending to me, so it will definitely rub Elizabeth raw.

Yes. Elizabeth is furious. "What's so funny?"

Kourtney remembers that she's condescending to someone who wants to gut her. "You don't really believe that do you?"

Elizabeth looks at her warily. "What do you mean?"

"He's going to have you and James kill yourselves and he won't do it." Kourtney says carefully, measuring her words and tone as if they are an old stick of dynamite that she's carrying.

"Why would he do that? He doesn't want to go to prison." This curiosity is unlike her. I wonder if I should step in.

"Like, of course not, but he'll be a celebrity forever. He'll become the Charles Manson of his generation. He'll have his following while you and James will be just like dead and stuff."

Elizabeth is the most annoyed that she's been all day. Echoes of Pompeii before the eruption. "You're forgetting something. He loves me."

Kourtney starts to laugh. "Oh my God, you think that psycho loves you? Why did he marry me then?"

"James picked that, not him!"

"What makes you think he didn't tell James to pick it? It's so obv James will do anything he says."

Elizabeth leans forward and bares her teeth. "Shut up now!"

Kourtney realizes that she's pushed her luck. She shuts up. Now.

33

I bring in the supplies and smile as I motion for James to turn on the camera and return me to my natural state of grace.

"We're back and with our now what is it thirty-four million viewers, James?"

"Thirty-five million now."

"Perfect," I say. "So, let's begin. Come here Kim."

Despite her stupidity even Kim can sense something is awry. "Um, please don't."

"Um, please do," I say, sing song.

"What are you going to do?"

"Just recreate your most famous picture that "broke the internet." We're going to break it this time too, but we're going to rape it first. "

"Like..." is all the idiot can mutter.

"Like get your stupid fucking cheek-implanted face over here." I shout.

Kim walks towards me slowly, like she's marching to a funeral.

Instead of the dress and gloves she wore for the photo Kim is wearing a trash bag and dishwater gloves.

Kim is crying, knowing the world will see her at her worst or what she perceives to be her worst. We all know we've seen her in situations much worse than this. She's the only one who seems unaware of this. She sobs as she speaks. "Like oh my god, this is so wrong."

I take a picture of it with Kim's phone. "Now it's going on your Instagram account."

Kim cries more. "Oh my God, no. You can't post that."

She is really doubling down on the inanity. "Idiot, the whole world is watching this. They've already seen it. It's just for good measure."

"Oh... yeah..."

"Well, we're not quite done yet. Now. Kim K., we need to have some fun. Lizzie B., want to take over?"

Elizabeth's eyes light up with joy as she grabs the knife with Kim's name on it. She grabs Kim by her hair and starts hacking it off.

Kim screams in pain.

I let out a loud laugh. "This is the sort of pain I feel knowing you're a fucking celebrity in our joke of a country." *That and more.*

Elizabeth continues to cut until Kim's hair is above her neck. It's a catastrophe and looks ridiculous. "You look fab!" says Elizabeth.

"She does, but we're not quite done," I say, watching Kim closely. It's time. I grab a gallon of milk from the refrigerator and dump it on Kim's head. She lets out another cry. I then pour the milk in Kim's mouth until she can't breathe. "That's how it's done. Now, we need another picture."

Elizabeth grabs Kim's phone and takes the picture. Kim cries in distress.

I'm trying to decide what to do next, nearly paralyzed with options. "Oh, yes. You had champagne too." I walk towards Kim and smash the champagne bottle on Kim's head. She falls to the floor.

Elizabeth raises her hands over her head like a cheerleader. "Selfie time," she says. She takes Kim's phone and snaps a picture of the two of them together. Elizabeth smiles absurdly while Kim is unconscious.

34

The cycle repeats, the cycle repeats. I'm on the phone talking to Waterman. He's still going on about Keanu Reeves. There's something soothing in the loony routine. My thoughts drift and I think of a song I listened to a few days ago. Run Mascara Run by the Raveonettes. A strangely beautiful song. I wonder why it came to mind now. I guess because they're actually talented and write great songs, but aren't known even 1 percent the way they should be. But we all know who the fucking Kardashians are don't we? Oh well, great song. Back to Waterman.

"We have Keanu in custody now."

"It doesn't matter. Mr. Keanu wanted that to happen." I say, as I'm completely used to this strange man now.

"That's what I thought. But you should know something. We had to take Sweet November off the air. We have had eight confirmed suicides since we started."

Only eight? I would have thought the number would be much higher. Oh well. "Good, now show the Lake House," I say, struggling to keep it together.

Waterman is screaming again. "What?! I can't do that! I just told you that we have eight confirmed suicides. If we play that it'll be least be twenty more!"

I hang up the phone laughing. As unbelievable as it all is, it continues to get crazier.

Meanwhile, Kourtney is still trying to convince Elizabeth I don't love her. I've decided to let her do her best, or worst. Whatever. "He just uses the two of you. Like you even more than James. He pretends like he loves you and stuff but he doesn't."

Elizabeth's discontent for these idiots is only growing. "Stop talking. Your voice sounds like a mix of a cat having its head cut off and Ben Stein working as a sex phone operator."

Kourtney is confused by this comment. "Um, like no? Anyway, you know he like doesn't love you. This is his show and you're just like the pawn thing."

Elizabeth turns to Kourtney, now giving her full attention. She looks at her aggressively, frightening Kourtney, who tries to conceal it while she continues. "Like, just listen and stuff. If he really did love you he wouldn't marry me, not even as a joke. Like, it would hurt him and stuff inside or whatever to even pretend to be with someone else."

In a bitter tone Elizabeth says, "Sacrifices have to be made for this cause. Even if that means marrying one of the dumbest and ugliest bitches on the planet."

Kourtney is upset and can't hide it. "So rude!"

Elizabeth gets closer to Kourtney's face. "Nothing you say can or will change how we feel about each other. We're soul-mates."

Kourtney lets out a loud laugh. "Oh my God. His soul-mate is the camera. He's totally using you. He's doing this for two reasons. A: Attention. And B: He loves Taylor Swift not you."

Now it's Elizabeth who's amused. Kourtney's attempt is pitiful to her. "I know he's a showman and I'm fine with it. It's one of the many reasons I love him. As for the Taylor Swift thing you're reaching so much it's pathetic."

"Did you look at the magazine he was looking at earlier?"

Elizabeth gets up to get the magazine. Elizabeth looks at it and sees Taylor Swift on the cover. She throws it and shouts, "So fucking what?"

Kourtney tries to think of something quickly. "Um, why do you think he picked us? He's like mad and stuff about Kanye ruining her moment."

"That's idiotic. Even for you," says Elizabeth.

Kim joins in now. "Actually, he told me that Swiffer is better than me and Kanye. So not true of course, though."

"You're a liar." Elizabeth is motionless.

Kim thinks for a moment. "No, like when you were bedazzling your knives (oh and by the way mine looks fab), he said so."

Elizabeth is starting to quiver. "What did he say? Word for word?"

Kim thinks again. She goes back to the horror chamber of her slut mind.

Finally, it's enough. I'm just done. "You're the most insipid couple on the face of the earth," I say. "Your idiotic husband is actually worse than you. From his prosaic lyrics, marrying you, and interrupting Beck and Taylor Swift. I've never encountered such banality in my entire life."

Kim replies slowly and stupidly. "Like Kanye told me he did it because he always interrupts women who aren't as pretty as me. But like he had to stop because he was interrupting *literary* every woman on earth because I'm the prettiest ever."

I shout, there's no way not to. "Good fucking God, idiot. The word is literally, buffoon. Oh and Taylor Swift is much prettier than you, but who isn't? Beck is even prettier than you and he's a guy. You have the body of an underdeveloped lumberjack who needs to be killed. Now shut the fuck up."

I'm still waiting in the kitchen. I decide to let this go on a little longer just to see what will happen.

Kim snaps back into reality. "Oh, I remember now. He said like literary or something that annoying blonde girl is prettier than everyone even me and um... Beck and a lumberjack should kill me or something and then a bunch of words I've never heard before."

Elizabeth looks at Kim, confused anew, agitated beyond measure.

Kourtney feels the need to clarify and with good reason. "What Kim is trying to say is like Eric wants her dead because he thinks Taylor is the prettiest woman ever and he thinks Beck and a lumberjack should kill her for being married to the guy who publicly insulted Taylor Swift."

Kim looks at Kourtney like she's a moron. "Uh, duh, I already said that."

Elizabeth is distraught now. She's convinced herself that it's true. She sits down on the couch to brace herself. "Come to think of it... I've never heard him insult her and he insults everyone. He made a comment about Kanye interrupting people earlier too. In front of me..."

"Yeah, totally," says Kim. "Paris Hilton totally has a body like Big Bird."

Kourtney looks at Kim, confused by the non sequitur. "We're talking about Taylor Swift. Not Paris Hilton."

"Oh, I don't know who that is," says Kim.

I decide to stay back because I know I'm going to laugh over the whole ridiculous thing. Quietly I remember one of the many letters I wrote to celebrities. I wrote one to Taylor Swift, didn't I? Well, good news because you're going to read it, dear reader!

Eric Ryder

Your Momentary Glamour Messiah
Riding a Black Horse as Prince Charming
In a Field of Bloody Dead Flowers, United States of America: Endless Fall of Rome
Myonlylovesprungfrommyonlyhate@theseviolentdelightshaveviolentends.com

August 21, 2016

Taylor Swift
The Forgotten Capulet
Narcissist in Training: Madonna's School of Narcissism and Sociopathy
Narcissistic Victim Ave. I Just Need a Prince South of Stop Bullying People
on Social Media

Dear Taylor,

I have to say I'm so disappointed in what's going on with you these days. What's happened? I remember when you first came out and you were the country girl (from the city) who was sweet. You were the girl all the clingy little girls who dream of having a perfect wedding could relate to. You were amazing then. You could turn yourself into a victim unlike anyone I've ever seen in my life. You were even trying to teach people to be better human beings. You even got to me a few times with that. When I was harrassing this guy online for being a redneck I thought about some of the things you said about bullying. I honestly did. I thought to myself is this wrong? Then I looked at his messages and noticed his status was, "Goin huntin wit daddy jerkey meat comin soon." Yeah, so I made shemale profile and sent him a message under it. Before I knew it he wanted to meet me for what he called, "Save the gay sex." He told me it isn't gay even if I have a penis because in my fancy pictures I look female so he can suck my penis. Anyway, I sent these messages to his family and of course they shunned him.

But, I did think about it before I bullied him. I wouldn't have even given it a second thought before that. So, I say thank you for that, Taylor.

Anyway, pretty girl. I lost my point there so I'm going to attempt to go back to it. So, you used to be the country girl from the city. You had soft, pretty, and curly blonde hair. You were an absolute treasure. But now? Now, oh dear Mithras. You seem like this awful mix of a Madonna wannabe and a weird Christian girl who lost her way. Wait, aren't the two the same thing? I don't know, but anyway... it works for Madonna. I even like Madonna. I hate her fucking music, but I do like the artistry of it all. I prefer the Thin White Duke, but I respect what she's doing even if I hate the music. But, Taylor... this isn't you. Is your career so important that you're willing to turn your back on who you are? Think about all the little girls who are dreaming of having an emotionally abusive boyfriend so they can play the victim. They need you, pretty girl. Where will they turn to when that boyfriend insults them and yells at them? They need your music to listen to while they're crying before he brings them roses so they can make up before he does it all over again.

My Mithras, Taylor. I think it's up to me. I really do, pretty girl. I'm going to end my current relationship with Kris Kardashian to be with you. Our child Glam-Glam Rydashian will just have to deal with the divorce like so many other children do. I can be your Romeo. Only I'll be your Romeo in the form of Dorian Gray. You'll be Juliet in the form of Sibyl Vane. Wait, that doesn't end too well for you if we do that, does it? Okay, I don't wish any harm to you so you'll just be Juliet and I'll be Dorian Gray disguised as Romeo. We'll take one of your little weird cats on a walk in the park and I'll hold your hand while we share an ice cream cone (that I'll later throw up because I'm not keeping that shit in my body). After that I'll respectfully kiss you on the cheek. A day later as our relationship progresses we can share an Eskimo kiss. After we break that humble embrace I'll get down on one knee and ask you to be my bride. You'll of course say yes. We'll be married that night and I'll look at your pretty face and quickly realize while I do find you attractive I just can't consummate the marriage. You're pretty, but there isn't any sexual attraction, dear. The innocence mixed with the victim mentality that I've helped restore to your very essence is just too much for me. I'd have to put a sleeping pill in your champagne and sneak out that night. I'd end up walking the streets of Hollywood and find another pretty lady who looks exactly like Elizabeth Banks. It isn't her (I fucking wish) but I'd pretend it is her. She's pretty too, but she's also awesome. She has a great sense of humor and is sexy as fuck. So, yeah, I'd consummate the sexiness of her or something. I am Dorian Gray disguised as Romeo. I'm all about me and the sexiness of Elizabeth Banks and all the women who look like her. By the way, why did they say she was too old to be in that shitty Spider-Man movie? I would have actually watched it if she were in it even though it sucked. Fuck, I would even watch every *Keeping Up with the Kardashians* episode if it were called *Keeping Up with the Sexiness of Elizabeth Banks*. Did you see that porn movie thing she was in that wasn't even actually porn? It was better than any real porn and she isn't even nude in it. That's fucking sexiness right there.

On second thought, Taylor. Forget everything I said before and do this one thing. Become Elizabeth Banks. We can consummate the marriage a billion times then.

Anyway, pretty girl. I hope you enjoy the show and will consider my proposal.

Sincerely yours,

Eric Ryder

35

I walk back in and see Elizabeth and Kourtney talking.

"What's wrong?" I ask, knowing full well.

Elizabeth stands up and walks towards me. "I need to talk to you. It's important."

I simply don't have time for this. "Not now, there's a reporter about to come in. He wants to interview us and get a look from the inside."

Elizabeth pleads with me, but I just can't be bothered. I can't allow it. It's a strength.. "It's really important, Eric."

"And this isn't?" There's an edge in my voice.

"Not as important, no." I don't like this challenge. I don't like it.

The doorbell rings. I look at Elizabeth and kiss her on the cheek. "As soon as it's over, I promise," I say walking away to answer the door.

Kourtney seizes the opportunity once more. "He doesn't seem to care much about how you feel."

Elizabeth says nothing. Kim gets up and touches Elizabeth's arm like a compassionate person would. But, she is Kim Kardashian and not a compassionate person. "OMG, I don't know why he wouldn't care about how you feel. Your skin feels totally great. What kind of lotion do you use? I so need the number of your skin guy."

36

I let the reporter in. It's Iggy Pop and I am rapturous. I feel like I'm going into shock. "It's an honor, sir," I say. "Raw Power is one of the greatest albums ever. It sounds like the soundtrack to an exorcism. It was before the contamination of the digital era."

Iggy smiles. "Thanks. It's good to know not everyone is a fan of the digital age."

"No, all of that is garbage. You can't feel the aggression, the passion, and there isn't any soul to any of it," I say.

Elizabeth joins in with wretchedness. "First Taylor Swift and now Iggy Pop is your guy crush?"

Iggy looks confused. "Taylor Swift?"

I whisper to Elizabeth. "Act properly." Implicit in the words is the *or else* that she knows will follow if she disobeys.

But Elizabeth lets fly. "Just one more person you love more than me."

"Stop it," I say softly.

Iggy sits down, waiting for me. I glare at Elizabeth before taking a seat.

Iggy starts the interview, the man with the plan. "I guess the first question is... why? Why go to such great lengths to do this?"

There's no reason to play it cool. I need to show him just how much I'm enjoying this. How proud I am of what I've accomplished and will accomplish. "Our society is mindless and the fact these imbeciles created a hit show while being the imbeciles they are is enough. It was time to take action."

"But why like this? Does it have to be violent?" Iggy asks.

"No, of course not. However, people don't want opinions like that. People only listen when you have a blade to their throats or to someone else's throat."

Iggy shrugs. "You don't think you'd matter without the violence?"

"Society wants action. Even if they disagree with it they respect it. They won't admit to it, but they do. Look at what you did early on in your career. It was insanity and it was brilliant." My heart pounds when I remember how unjustly he was treated. What. Is. Wrong. With. People?

"I appreciate that, but, what's made the music last wasn't the stage antics. It's the music and fire behind it," Iggy says

"That's certainly true. But, we have a message too and that's ultimately what's going to stick. The message is what's fueling the insanity.

"I can understand that. But I don't recall ever holding people at gunpoint no matter how stupid they are. So, why that?" says Iggy.

"The Marquis de Sade is a good example. He wrote about rape, pedophilia, and extreme violence, and despite being hated we're intrigued by him. He's still being studied today and so will I two hundred years from now."

Iggy looks interested. "The Marquis de Sade? So you like to read?"

I nod. "I do. One of the many reasons I'm sitting here. Look at what our country has become. More people know who the Kardashians are than Sylvia Plath. All forms of art are dying in this country."

"How do you mean?"

"People would rather watch superhero movies and pretend they're twelve again than have to deal with real emotions. We went from Gone with the Wind to some nonsense about Superman."

"That's interesting. I don't even disagree. Do you believe it's beyond repair?" Iggy asks with interest.

"Yes, it is. Basically, the work we're doing here in the long-term is pointless. At least in terms of how society will view it."

"Then why do it?"

"I want the world to know that not everyone is scared to feel something. More importantly, I'm not scared to act on what I feel. Surely you can understand what I'm feeling."

Iggy nods, and it's all the vindication I think I've ever wanted. "I feel exactly the way you do. I just don't know about the methods is what I'm saying."

I smile before I respond. "This is my poetry."

Iggy laughs. Man, when Iggy Pop thinks you're a trip you're really on to something. He turns to Elizabeth. "What about you, Elizabeth? We haven't talked to you yet. You really seem to like knives."

"Elizabeth loves her knives," I say with affection. "I think even more than she loves me."

Elizabeth is somber. "No, Eric. I don't love anyone or anything more than you."

Something is truly wrong. There's been a real shift here that I haven't given enough gravity to. I have to make it right and walk it back. "Well, I'm glad to hear that. I hope you know that I feel the same."

I turn back to Iggy. He's asked another question but Elizabeth interrupts him. "Do you, Eric?"

I look back at Elizabeth with suspicion. "I would hope you know that."

Elizabeth smiles and I'm a little relieved to see she responds properly. Iggy and I go back to the interview. Still smiling, Elizabeth gets up and walks towards the two of us.

Iggy looks at her, grins, and widens his eyes while leaning back. "So, Elizabeth. What's your reason for doing this?"

Elizabeth smiles calmly at me, then at Iggy. Then, very casually, she pulls out a pistol and shoots Iggy in the head. I jump from the chair in total shock.

37

I scream in horror and shock, and a hideous mixture of a million other emotions I won't   able to decipher without time and tears. "What the hell are you doing?! That's Iggy fucking Pop!"
Elizabeth asks, "Why the Kardashians?"

"What?! What?" All I can do is scream. And scream. And then for good measure, to scream it again.

Elizabeth repeats the question, as if I'm some fool, and suddenly I feel like I am. "Why did you pick the Kardashians!"

I ignore her. "You just killed Iggy Pop!" Iggy had survived just about everything the world could throw at a person, and of all things he had died of it's Elizabeth.

Elizabeth folds her arms across her chest, still clutching the gun in one hand. "Are you sure there isn't someone else?"

The question rattled me, both with its irrelevance and its import. "What the fuck are you talking about?"

"You say you love me, but you married a woman you hate as a joke. You must think I'm an even bigger joke. Well I'm no joke!"

I sure as hell am not laughing. "Dear God, Elizabeth. Do you want me to kill her now to prove to you how little she means to me?"

"That isn't the point." She unfolded her arms and jabbed the gun in my direction. "If you loved me you would never make a mockery out of marriage."

"Marriage and love in most cases have nothing to do with one another."

Elizabeth narrows her eyes. "You always have an answer. Let me ask you something else, though. You said you'd kill Kourtney for me."

Thank God. Something I understand. "Yes, shall I do it?"

"Would you kill Taylor Swift for me?"

"What are you talking about?" I say beyond all motherfucking shock.

"Oh my god, look at him trying to avoid the question," she says. Elizabeth casts her eyes heavenward, pleading to understand me, when in fact there was only one answer: she was far crazier than I had known. "We know, Eric."

"Know fucking what?" There's nothing that I am so poorly equipped to deal with as another person's smugness.

"You're doing this to try and impress Taylor Swift because she's the one you love."

"I knew you were a lunatic but this takes it to another fucking planet."

Elizabeth chews her lip, remembering some asinine enterprise. "I remember that one time you played her music to annoy rednecks online and we both laughed. But, you were really doing it for yourself."

Kourtney whoops, feeling the balance shift. "Totally, it's why he insisted he be able to talk to Kanye. He's super mad at him for interrupting his dream girl's speech and stuff."

As if from a great height, I watch myself go towards Kourtney and hold my gun against her head. "What else do you have to say?"

Elizabeth points the gun at my head.

I'm not even remotely scared and I turn to face her fully. "Do it. You've already ruined this interview, so you might as well ruin the entire thing. Fucking do it!"

Elizabeth backs off a little scared of my reaction. I'm not sure what she was expecting. Tears? Groveling? A declaration of love?

"You just took my most brilliant moment away from me," I say.

Now she's angry. She's forgetting that she should be scared.

"Your most brilliant moment should have something to do with me."

"It does, you're here!"

"No, not like that you prick! I do everything for you. I even do my make-up like you want me to! You told me to look like a macabre doll and I fucking do it. Everything I do is for you." As if to demonstrate this for everyone, she leans over and smacks herself on the ass.

I'm whispering, and hate that I'm trying to hide anything, from anyone, especially this crew. "Shut up, you don't tell anyone that."

"You even had me wear exact dresses when you were fucking me!" Her eyes widen.

"I know why now! That dress you made me buy. It's exactly like I've seen Taylor Swift wear.

"You're insane! You know what, it doesn't matter right now. We have more to do. I can't believe you killed Iggy fucking Pop. I can't even look at you and your mess. Clean it up. James, help her so we can move this along."

James coughs into his hand. "Are you serious? I just cleaned up the other mess."

"I don't know, James. Do I look like I'm being humorous?"

"Fine." James grinds his teeth as he leaves the room to get a mop. He's feeling a new kind of hate for me right now and I simply don't have the time to deal with it at the moment.

"Set up the camera, Elizabeth," I say. "Let's get this over with."

38

Elizabeth sets up the camera while I clear my throat, arrange my thoughts, and get ready to plunge back in. "Welcome back everyone," I say. "I'd like to thank you for voting. However, we're going to have a twist with this time." In my head I can hear the audience gasp. I've got them eating out of my hand, each and every one of them, fanned out across the country.

Kourtney, as ever, remains unconvinced and stymied. "You're probably faking the votes and picking what you want."

It's not really something I could put on a resume, but I'm truly impressed by my ability to stay completely calm while walking over and then slapping her. She's probably used to it by now, but the thrill is still there for me. "Elizabeth, dear. Please bring out our surprise."

Elizabeth is positively deranged with euphoria. "Certainly." She leaves the room, then returns with a woman who is gagged and bound.

Kim tosses her head around like a spastic toddler. "Like, oh my god…who's that?"

Beaming, I say, "This is Amanda. I doubt that she's pleased to meet you."

"Why is she here?" says Kim.

"She's part of the game, dear," I say.

"Just let her go," says Kourtney, assuming the mantle, arbiter of reality.

"That can happen," I say, "but unfortunately it isn't up to me. If it were she would be free by now."

Kourtney grimaces. "It's *all* up to you." She's not wrong, and it's so nice to hear her acknowledge it. Still, rules are rules.

"Actually, it's up to you three this time," I say.

"What do you mean?" says Khloe.

I can't help but smirk. "It's simple. The three of you get to vote this time."

Kim sighs with relief and pleasure. "Do we like, get to vote on how she dies and stuff?"

"Why would you want her to die?" says Kourtney. "Oh my god, that's so bad."

"Um," says Kim, "I was like joking. It's so obv."

"Why would you like joke that way?" says Kourtney. "You just saw someone die."

"Oh, yeah. I forgot!" says Kim, going full on defensive mode.

"Enough," I say, and truer words have never been spoken. "We're not going to separate you this time. I want to see your reactions to the answers" I point at Kourtney. "Who would you pick to die? Amanda or you?"

"Um, what? I'm not picking that. You're going to kill us all anyway."

"I'll make a deal with all three of you," I say. "If two of you pick Amanda to die instead of yourselves then Killing the Kardashians resumes and one of you will still get to live. However, you have to watch Amanda die." Squirm, ladies, squirm.

I look over to check with Elizabeth and am surprised to see her glaring at me like I'm…well, almost like I'm a Kardashian.

"So like what happens if we pick ourselves?" says Kourtney.

"If two of you pick to die instead of Amanda, then she's allowed to go free and unharmed." I'm still a little unnerved by Elizabeth's glowering. "The downside is, of course, you all die. Oh, I forgot to mention that when one of you votes, then the two other sisters will have a chance to try and sway the one who's voting."

Kim raises her hand.

"Do you have a question, Kimberly?" I say, ever the concerned instructor.

"Yeah, like is this going to take long? Because I have a meeting with my psychic tonight."

Of course she does. I wonder why her psychic didn't see me coming the last time they spoke? "I don't know. Should we read your horoscope and see what it says?"

She lights up like a Roman Candle. "OMG, fab idea. I'm a Libra. What are you? I bet you're a Pisces because you're actually kind of sweet in a serial killer way."

New depths. New surprises. New lows. I can only shake my head in astonishment as I look at Kim. To distract myself from Kim's maddening compliment I walk towards Amanda and remove the tape from her mouth with a satisfying ripping noise. "Anyway... before you vote, Kourtney, let's learn a little about Amanda. Tell us about yourself Amanda. Do you have any kids?"

"I have a daughter, Carol."

Kim laughs.

"What's funny, Kimberly?" I ask.

"I'm sorry, but you gave her a fat girl's name. She's so going to be fat! You doomed her and stuff."

Amanda's eyes go hard. "It was my mother's name."

"Was your mother fat?" says Kim.

Kim has utterly confused Amanda. I get it. Oh, I empathize, as much as I'm able. "What's wrong with you?" says Amanda.

"Stop it, Kim," says Kourtney.

"I'm sorry, but it's true," says Kim.

Kim, always pursuing the truth at all costs. Sigh. "Anyway, how old is your daughter, Amanda?" I say.

"She's seven."

"That's all for now. Remember what I told you earlier," I say.

Amanda nods. Smart girl. Much smarter than the Kardashians.

"So, Kourtney," I say. "Pick. Who dies, you or Amanda?

"You're despicable."

Maybe. But it changes nothing. "Pick now or you all die one by one."

"I *should* die," says Kourtney.

Khloe moans. "Oh my God, you have kids too, Kourt."

"Yeah, like you have two or... three?" says Kim. "I don't know, but I do know you have more than her, so you should pick her over yourself."

"No, I can't," says Kourtney. "There will be other people to make sure my kids have good lives. I pick me, that's my final vote."

This pleases me so greatly that I fight the urge to burst into song, any song. "You're up, Khloe."

"Oh my God, I don't want to pick."

I believe her. I don't care. "Well, here we can learn a little more about Amanda while you're thinking." Hopefully the act of thinking will not give her an aneurysm, ending the game before it's at its conclusion.

"Good idea," says Khloe.

I laugh. I've laughed more in the past twenty four hours than in the past year. "So, Amanda. What do you do for a living?"

"I'm a beautician."

Kim honks like a goose. "Oh my God, she's a peasant."

Elizabeth titters along with the honking bitch.

"So rude, like shut up, Kim," says Kourtney.

So," I say, "if you were to die, would you be leaving much money behind?

"No, none," says Amanda. "She has Cerebral Palsy and can't walk. All of the money goes to her physical therapy."

"You sound like a wonderful mother. It's honestly a complete pleasure to even know you." Certainly not the kind of mother you'd want to choke. No. Not at all.

Khloe appears as though she's about to cry.

"So, you don't have any kids, right?" I ask Khloe, hoping to turn off the spout before it starts.

"Not that she knows of," says Kim.

"Oh my God, I think I'd know Kim," says Khloe. "That only applies to men. But, no. I was pregnant once but the doctor said I had so much whiskey and vodka I drowned the baby and it died and stuff before I could give birth to it or whatever."

Yes. Or whatever. "So, who do you have in your life? Some basketball player husband who cheated on you? Who could blame him? He's successful for actually having talent and doing something that takes actual dedication. You're... well the Pig and nothing more." I say.

Khloe starts to cry. "You're right, I don't have anyone. I pick me."

"Is that your final vote?" I say.

"Wait," says Kim, "I get to try and change her mind."

Yes. Good girl. "You certainly do. By all means, go ahead." I cede the floor to her.

"Okay," says Kim, "like I know you're just the fat Kardashian and it isn't likely any guy will ever love you for you. But you're still a Kardashian and while you're not skinny and pretty your last name is the same as me and Kourt's so it gives you the illusion of being skinny and pretty. Well, kinda. So because of us, mostly me, you like have a lot of reasons to live."

The heart weeps.

Khloe stops crying. "That's the nicest thing you've ever said to me."

Khloe and Kim try to hug while being tied up, with dubious results.

"No, Khloe," says Kourtney. "Think about how we felt when dad died. Her daughter will feel the same."

"Oh..." The wheels are turning in Khloe's head. Slowly, but turning.

"No," says Kim, "but it hurt us so much because our dad was a Kardashian. He was like, special and stuff like us...but mostly me," she says, her voice dropping to a whisper.

"Oh, thanks, Kim," says Khloe. "I pick her, final vote."

"Oh my God, no..." Kourtney whimpers.

My God. You'd think that they'd be used to their own failures by now. "I'm sorry, but you had your chance and you failed."

Time to return to Amanda. My instincts for this are getting better with every moment. "Now, Amanda. If you were to die who would take care of Carol? Could her father?" I can't lie. I don't want her to be able to say yes. However, I already knew the answer to the question. Still, it's so much more exciting while on the air.

"No," says Amanda.

Perfect!

"He died in a car wreck. I don't know... no one would get her. I was an only child and all of my family is gone other than distant relatives. I don't think they'd take her with the financial responsibility involved."

"How sad," I say.

I walk back towards Kim. "You're up, dear."

Kim clucks her tongue as if she can't believe I don't already know what she's about to do. "It's so obv, I pick her."

"You're truly the biggest narcissist ever." I can almost admire it. If there's one thing I never wanted to be, it was *merely* anything. The biggest winner, loser, killer, lover, torturer, star, anything but mere. I think Kim gets it, even though she would never be able to articulate it.

"Kim," says Kourtney, "it's like she said... our kids will be okay. They have their fathers and will have good lives.

"Wait, can I change my vote?" says Khloe.

"No, it's too late," I say. "What do you say Kim?"

"Um, sorry," says Kim, looking anything but, "but it isn't just my kids who need me. I have fans too and they're a lot like kids so I have literally like a trillion kids. Her, the mother with the fat kid. That's my final vote."

The thought of her bereaved, abandoned fans is the least moving thing I can picture. It's time. I move to Amanda, lean down, whisper into her ear (something none of you need to know), and then shoot her in the head. It's a burst of such exquisite pleasure that I nearly black out. To think, they forced my finger to pull the trigger. I didn't kill that poor mother, they did.

39

When I return to something like reality Elizabeth is irate and screaming. What on earth has gotten her so worked up? The gun is still warm in my hand.

"How could you?" She flutters her hands like they're little dying birds.

Of all the things I expected from her this was the last. "We talked about this before. You knew this was part of the plan." Loyalty. Harder and harder to come by. One of the problems with being reliable is that you start to expect it of everyone else.

"I know why you did it."

Of course she does, the twit. She's known all along. What wild epiphany does she think she's having? "It was part of the game."

"No, I know the real reason. It's because she looks like Taylor Swift." Elizabeth steps back and makes fists, unclenches them, clenches them again.

Dear God. "Well, I didn't think it was possible, but I guess it is." I've never spent much time regretting my choices, but Elizabeth...dear God.

"That I would figure it out? I did."

"No," I say. "That a Kardashian doesn't hold the title of stupidest person here. Congratulations, you've achieved something that I didn't even know was possible." Wonder of wonders. Miracle of miracles. Idiot of idiots.

Now she's running towards me. Now she's got her hand at the sheath in her belt. Now she's got a knife to my throat. Now she's getting too tedious for words.

"Don't think you can get out of this by making me think I'm stupid."

I lean down, deliberately pressing my neck into the edge of the blade. Her eyes go to the blood, she's worried. "Oh, I don't. You're too dumb to see the truth, so we're stuck here in this everlasting moment of stupidity with the Whoredashians as your personal cheerleaders."

"Stop it! Stop!"

"So, let me ask you something, dear. If I'm in love with Taylor Swift, a fucking celebrity I don't know on any level, why did I kill someone who supposedly looks like her?"

"I know how you work. First you picked her because she looks like her. Then after I figured it out and called you out on it, you had to set it up where she'd die. That way you could pretend like it isn't true. Then you would think I would think, 'Oh, he really doesn't love her cause he killed a woman who looks like her.'"

"I take it back. You're not stupid. You're insane." Not that I didn't know this. I've just preferred her insanity to be on my terms.

"Oh, is that the way it is? So you're not in love with Taylor Swift?" She says this as if it's an old, tired argument we've been having our whole lives.

"How can I be in love with someone I don't know?" Especially when it's basically impossible for me to love anyone that I *do* know.

Elizabeth considers this. "Okay, so you're telling me if I cut off Amanda's face and put it over my face you wouldn't want to fuck me right now?"

"Yeah, I can honestly say I wouldn't." I reply with a slight laugh. What a fucking amazing question.

Elizabeth pushes the blade in a little deeper, still without cutting me. "Liar."

"Do it." I push against it again, harder than she's willing to. She relents and takes some of the pressure off the blade.

"Bastard!" Elizabeth pulls the blade away from my throat. I know the smirk on my face must be torture for her.

"Aw," I say, "you must love me as much as I love Taylor Swift."

"OMG," bleats Kourney. "Do you have like any empathy for anyone at all?"

"OMG that would be so great!" Kim is rapturous. "I think we have some in the kitchen."

"What?" Kourtney sounds like she'd be tearing her hair out if she wasn't tied up.

"Uh, where else would the cookies be, Kourt? Duh." Kim stares at the ceiling, her lips moving wordlessly with her non-thoughts.

"So, dear," I say to Elizabeth, "have you decided to rejoin me in reality or are you still in Whoredashianland?"

A tear runs down her cheek. "Why can't you just love me the way you love Taylor Swift?" She runs across the room and pushes herself against a wall.

"Oh Jesus fucking Christ. Do you even realize how ridiculous you are?" I'm shouting, moving towards her, not sure what I'm going to do when I reach her.

Then there's something over my mouth. A rag, clutches in James's hand. Before I can fight I know that I'm passing out.

40

When I come to, I'm in the kitchen, tied to the table. I'm aware that I'm a captive in the same instant that I'm conscious, and I thrash with fury. Not this, not now, no changes at the end! That fucking James. Oh God, when I get off of this table…but they've really tied me up and I exhaust myself quickly.

I can raise my head enough to see Elizabeth trotting around the room, examining her tools. Kim it as her side, the happy, oblivious assistant.

"What the fuck are you doing?" My throat nearly bursts with the force of my scream.

"Darling, you're awake!" Elizabeth chirps and prances like it's the morning after our wedding night, not like she's tied me down and done who knows what.

"Untie me now."

"In a minute, darling. We're almost done. I just have to clean you up first."

Knowing Elizabeth, that can't mean anything good. "What are you talking about?"

Elizabeth approaches and takes my hand. She opens her mouth halfway and hesitates. "Darling, I'm a lesbian now."

"What? With whom? Kim?" Indignity after indignity.

"God no! With Erica."

At least it's not Kim. "Who is Erica?"

"You, silly!"

Kim rushes over like I just unwrapped a shiny donut. I realize that I'm numb. I can't feel as much of my body as I should be able to. "OMG, Erica," says Kim. "You're so going to love your new life. Caitlyn totally does. She told me it was fun to ride four wheelers before, but nothing is better than riding them in a skirt."

I can't imagine what this has to do with me, but Kim is no stranger to sentences that don't connect.

Elizabeth finishes whatever she's doing, cleaning up her work. She casually cuts me free with a deft stroke of her blade. Something's wrong. I steel myself, then sit up and look down at myself.

"I'm sorry, darling," says Elizabeth. "But it was necessary and now we can be together, free of your naughty thoughts about Taylor. We fixed you."

But I wasn't broken. As I look at the mess of blood, at the spot where I—where whatever it was that made me a man used to be—I'm surprised by how calm I am. "We?"

"Kim read the directions to me from her phone!"

"I did!" says Kim. "OMG, when does his vagina grow in? I wonder if Caitlyn has hers yet."

The last thing I want to think about is growing a vagina. "Elizabeth, what good does this do? I didn't have any plans to use my penis before killing myself, anyway." What is she playing at?

Elizabeth studies me like Nabokov might have looked at one of his innumerable butterflies. "I had to make sure that during what time we have left together you wouldn't have naughty thoughts about Taylor."

"I never had thoughts about her at all!"

"It doesn't matter now. It's over and now we're lesbians together, Erica."

I'm not a lesbian. "My name is not Erica."

"It's okay, you'll make a great lesbian with me. We'll be the prettiest lesbian couple ever."

"Totally, Erica, you're a way prettier woman than Khloe," says Kim.

I know I said I was crazy, but I was wrong. For the first time I feel like I'm actually losing my mind. "Shut up you fucking idiots! No matter what you've done, I'm still a man."

"It's okay, it's all behind us now."

"Totally," says Kim. "The sooner you accept it the better off you'll be and stuff. I just want you to know I support transgender people. When Bruce became Caitlyn I was the first to get her shoes. I didn't even get mad when I found out she was the reason my lingerie smelled like male parts."

"I'm not transgender you nitwit!" In any possible permutation of the multiverse, the conversation occurring makes more sense than this one.

"OMG, Erica," says Kim. "Make up your mind."

Elizabeth motions for Kim to stop talking. "It's okay, we're going to be happy now," she says. "We're meant to be."

I'm starting to calm down, vaguely wondering when my surgery might start to hurt.

"I'll deal with you in a minute. Where the fuck is James? I need to take care of him."

"Oh, about that. He had the wrong idea." She shrugs, as if we're talking about a bill that didn't get paid in time.

"Tell me."

"Well, after he knocked you out, I had him help me tie you up. You were heavy!"

"Sorry," I say. "Tell me."

"Well," she says, "as soon as we got you tied up, he decided it was confession time or something. Got all weird. It took about five seconds before he says 'I'm so glad you realized what he is, Elizabeth.'"

"What's that supposed to mean?" I say.

"That's what *I* said," she says. "I just went, '*what*?' Then he moved in closer and said, like he was all smooth, 'He never loved you the way I do.'"

I start laughing. This is all so very James.

"Tell me about it," she says. "I just looked at him forever and said, 'You... love me?' Then he puts on this deep voice and makes the speech." Elizabeth clears her throat. 'Elizabeth, I've loved you from the moment I saw you. Eric tied you up since you were trying to kill the neighbor because she talked to him. Even with duct tape over your mouth, you were the most beautiful woman I ever saw.'"

"And then?" I say.

"I was sweet. I said that I wished I'd known sooner, and I meant it, just not for the reason he thought. I gave him a hug and it was like he'd reached Heaven."

"And then?"

She smiles. "Then I stabbed in the back. He died."

I growl. "That should have been my kill."

She looks truly penitent. "I'm sorry, darling. Are we okay now? I hope you know I only did this for our relationship."

The sweet fool. "Listen, I'm fucking pissed you would do this. But with that said, you know I love you and I certainly know you love me. Let's just make the most of the time that we have left together. I don't want to spend it fighting."

"Oh, darling."

I reach out my hand, which she takes with a smile. But when she tries to move forward with me, striding towards our blissful, if brief, future together, I pull her back. I grab her from behind and choke her with crushing force. Over Elizabeth's shoulder I watch Kim cry and cover her eyes, and it's a ridiculous thrill when she peeks between her fingers for a look.

"Did you think I would allow you to get away with humiliating me?" I hiss in Elizabeth's ear. "Did you think you wouldn't pay for it? Did you think I would be forgiving? You wanted my attention, you wanted my love? Now you have it."

She tries to fight back, but it's useless. Within seconds I drop her dead body to the floor with a thump.

I look at her and down to the blush of the bosom I'm tangled to the ivory of her stripped ink. Forever on a bed of rogue she's like a celibate maiden dawning Elysia in her fair ichor. More beautiful in death than in life. Had I known her collapse would be this lucent I'm not sure I wouldn't have killed her on the first night we met. Oh, my love... if only you could have lived as beautifully as you died.

If this were a movie (which it will be and Henry Rollins should still play Lieutenant Waterman), this is just the spot where you'd get the fade to black, which would then fade back in in the living room, with a rather dejected-looking version of me sitting in a chair, then jumping slightly as the phone rings.

"Hello?" I say.

It's Waterman, out by the gate somewhere. Out in the safe world where people don't try to turn their partners into lesbians to end imaginary affairs with Taylor Swift. But they do think Keanu Reeves runs the Illuminati or something... I guess.

"You motherfucker! We've been calling nonstop! We're coming in now."

"If you were coming in you would have done it already." He knows it. I know it. What the hell are we pretending for?

"No you little fuck, we are."

"Do it and see what happens."

He makes a gagging sound. "It was one thing when you bastards killed the Iggy Pop, but a fucking mother! Where did you have her?"

"We brought her in with us and put her in a closet. And I didn't kill her. Kim did."

"You pulled the trigger, you fuck."

"We're almost done." In every sense of the word, *Lieutenant.*

I hang up on his new round of screams. I get to my feet and give the Kardashians a weary look.

"Um," says Kim, "like, can you stop that? It's kind of freaky."

"The time has come," I say.

"The time for like what?" says Kim.

"Death." I point the gun at her head.

"No, no! You didn't do the vote and stuff!"

"But we did. I knew you'd fuck it up and make me do something I didn't want to do. I set it up before you even knew Amanda existed."

Kim closes her eyes. "No, no, no, no."

Yes, yes, yes. I quickly pull the gun away from Kim's head and shoot Khloe. Kim opens her eyes and isn't sure if she should cheer for being alive or scream because she's covered in her sister's blood. So she does both. Kourtney screams, a hysterical, discordant chorus. The phone rings again and I answer it amidst the cacophony.

"Try anything and you'll have three dead Kardashians instead of two," I say into the phone.

God-fucking-Jesus-goddamn-motherfucking-cocksucking-Christ!"

"You've already lost your job over this, but do you want them all dead?"

"Listen, you little fucking prick! I don't care what happens, I will get you back for making me look like an ass. I don't care if you die before I get to you! I'll rape your fucking corpse, cut your asshole off your body with my seed in it, and send it to Kris Jenner." Waterman's indecorous collapse is as entertaining as his threats are impotent.

"Wait, what? Why would she want that?"

"To hang up over the mantle...I don't know! Do you think I became Lieutenant by thinking? Shoot first, think second, cover up third!"

"Good luck covering this one up."

He's screaming yet again when I hang up, yet again.

In the living room, the remaining two Kardashians clean up their sister's blood. It puts me in a better mood, not just the fact that they're laboring, but this particular labor.

"Kourt, you missed some brain there." I nod my head in the direction of the gray scrap.

"Like, oh my God," says Kourtney.

"All right, that's enough," I say. I walk over, pull them both up by their hair, and make them sit down again. "One last game."

"Do you ever stop?" says Kourtney.

I ignore her. It barely even takes effort at this point. "You two had one awful father, no?"

"Oh my god," says Kim. "Our father was amazing."

Kourtney sneers at me. "Yeah, you would be lucky to be one percent of the man he was."

"He helped keep a man out of prison everyone knew was guilty. So in reality, your father was worse. He cared more about doing his job than finding justice."

"Oh my God," says Kourtney, "look what you're doing here. Can you really talk?

They misunderstand. Of course they do. It must be an exhausting way to live. "Who's to say I think it's a bad thing?"

My little dummies look confused.

"I do realize you're both morons. But, the fact remains that the two of you have his blood running through your veins."

"Totally. I have his hair, too." Kim whips her hair around like she's in a music video.

"Well," I say, "if he could even help get the Juice off then surely one of you could save yourself."

"Um, I don't know," says Kim. "I threw out his law books a long time ago. They were taking up space for my selfie scrapbook."

One more laugh, for old time's sake. "You'll each defend yourselves and tell me and the viewers why the other should die. Whoever wins gets to live. Let the trial begin." I wish I had a gavel to bang. I settle for stomping my foot with a bang, making everyone jump.

Kim and I retire to her bedroom for the interview.

41

Kim sits on a chair. I sit on the bed across from her.

"Why should you live and why should Kourtney die?" Might as well keep it simple.

"It's so obv. I made this family so I get to live and like my kid or supposed kids are better looking than her kids because they came from me."

"Wow, those are brilliant reasons."

"Totally."

"But why should Kourtney die?

"Oh, this is so easy. You know what her and Khloe did once?

"What, dear?"

Kim blows air out of her cheeks. "So like, they were talking about this annoying girl named Nancy. They kept saying how annoying and selfish she is and kind of a bitch or something. So I was like, oh my God, who is this Nancy person? She sounds super annoying. Do you know who Nancy was?"

"Please tell."

Kim taps herself on top of the head. "Me! They were like talking about me the entire time in front of me but calling me Nancy and like I didn't have a clue!"

"What bitches."

"I know, right? Actually, now that I think about it, Khloe kind of deserved to die. Like, who would do that to their sister, especially the sister who made her famous?"

"Only a terrible person."

"Totally. Like, could you do the push on the stomach thing, what's it called? It like brings dead people back to life."

Kim Kardashian, Lazarus-level hopeful. "You want me to resuscitate someone who was shot in the head?"

"Yeah, like is that possible?" Kim asks with hope in her eyes.

I put my hand over my mouth. When I regain my composure I say, "I'm afraid not, dear. But why would you want to do that?"

"I want to tell her what a bitch she is for the whole Nancy thing her and Kourtney did. Then after I do, you could kill her again. I mean, like really... Someone who would do that to me kind of deserves to die twice."

Now she's speaking my language. "Wow, now you're impressing me. If only that were possible. Believe me, I'd be all for it."

"Maybe you could like call in a guy to do the freezing thing they do? You know, the Walt Disney death thingy."

Ah yes. Didn't someone win the Nobel Prize for the Walt Disney Death thingy? "Well, you've made quite the case for yourself. Your father would be proud. Hell, even uncle O.J. would be proud."

"Do you think I'm going to win?" Kim leans forward, as if we're partners in some fun prank.

"I don't know, but I'll certainly vote for you."

"Oh my God, if I win by one vote you're SO going to be my new BFF!"

We wrap it up and I bring Kourtney in to plead her case.

She is furious over Kim's reason as to why she should die. It's only fair that she gets a chance to respond in kind.

"So why should Kim die?" I say.

"Soooo many reasons. Like, have you seen her crying face? It's so awful and she looks so ugly."

"Yes, unfortunately anyone who uses the Internet has come across it." Kim's crying face would look right at home on the *Planet Earth* documentary, maybe in the episode about the freakish fish that live down so deep in the ocean that they have no concept of light.

"Also, this one time she had a total meltdown when one of her three hundred ex-husbands threw her in the water and she lost her earring. She started to cry and threw a fit."

"She cried over losing earrings?"

"Yeah, they were like seventy-five thousand dollars, but she made like seventy-five million from her stupid sex tape, so who cares? She made everyone look for them for over an hour. When no one could find them she went into the hotel room crying. But before that she complained about how awful the room was."

"What a fascinating individual. Anything else?"

"Oh, she also hates Ireland, like all of it. Even the part that's like not Ireland. Jr. England or whatever it's called. Anyway, like she went there and thought it was boring because she wouldn't leave her hotel. She thought like leprechauns would attack her for her gold or whatever. So like she hired someone to make a fake Twitter account to post that she hates Ireland. Then she later acted like it was fake. She did it because she wanted everyone to know she hates Ireland, but in case everyone gets too upset she can say she didn't post it and it was a fake account. Then like when she was robbed in Paris and stuff she was totally convinced the leprechauns snuck out of Ireland and robbed her or like Paris is now part of Ireland. Now she totally won't leave California because she's never seen leprechauns in California so like it must mean California pays the leprechaun tax to keep them out and stuff. Also, she loves even bad publicity. Like obviously."

"Wow, just wow." I'm sure Ireland is just heartbroken. If only Oscar Wilde were alive.

"I'm not done yet, though."

I thought not. "By all means, continue."

"Kim convinced Khloe that she was a lesbian when Khloe was about eighteen. She told Khloe she was bigger than us because she has more testosterone and stuff. Khloe ended up dating a chick for a while who kind of looked like a guy and was a truck driver. Khloe couldn't figure out why she didn't find feminine women attractive and only liked the ones who looked like guys."

"Please, you're joking."

"No, I'm totally serious. Kim talked her into trying to have sex with a woman too. So like, Khloe tried to sleep with her girlfriend and she ended up leaving because the woman smelled so bad. But Kim told her she just needed to find a cleaner woman and she'd like it. So Khloe thought she was a lesbian for two more years after that."

I can't help it. I jump to my feet for a standing ovation. "Brava, brava."

42

Back to the living room, then, to deliberate matters of life and death. In these last moments I find that I'm still capable of nerves. It feels like everything has been building to this, and I hope I'm up to it. Of course I'm up to it. "Wow, I just..."

"Just tell us."

"To my complete surprise..."

Kim and Kourtney look at something behind me and their faces go pale. Kourtney looks away, obviously trying to make me think that nothing's wrong. But Kim screams. She can't ever pass up a chance to get loud.

"OMG, zombie!" she says.

Of all the things she might have yowled, that was probably the last I would have chosen. Might as well look, though. I turn around to find James pointing a gun at me with steady hands.

Kourtney yells at Kim. "Idiot! He could have helped us! You gave him away."

"Uh, no. He's totally a zombie and stuff and zombies are like, bad." She rolls her eyes, mortified at Kourtney's ignorance.

James looks like he wants to see me squirm. "I saw what you did to her. You never loved her, but I always did." Oh good grief, this old, sad story. You'd think he'd get tired of being pathetic. Besides, didn't Elizabeth stab this douche, too?

James tries to pull the trigger but can't. He tries again and it still doesn't work. I figure I'll give him one more chance, but the boy just can't catch a break. He watches in confusion while I walk over and disarm him.

"Here," I say, taking the gun from him, "the safety is on."

James nods. "Thanks."

"No problem." I raise the gun and shoot him in the head. This small interruption over, I head back to the computer to read the results. "The winner, and the one who gets to live, is Kim."

Kim claps. I'm sure she never had a moment of doubt.

"Like, oh my god," she says. "Okay, so I'd like to thank all my awesome fans out there, Mom for voting me, and like mostly myself for being such an awesome lawyer. I was even better than Dad!"

"You're not receiving an award," I say.

"Oh..." She's sulking. Sullen.

"But you do get to live."

"Oh!" Kim claps again. "I shouldn't be so surprised. I mean, hello. I am awesome. BTW, Kanye and I can make it to dinner tomorrow night with you and Chris Brown."

Oh goody. "What do you have to say, Kourtney?"

Kourtney, for once, says nothing.

"Well, okay," I say, a little disappointed in her, "here's how it's going to work..."

"Stop talking and just do it," says Kourtney.

"I'm afraid that isn't how it works," I say. "So Kim, are you ready to do this?"

"Um, like do what?" Kim's mind was elsewhere, surprise, surprise.

"If you were to guess, what do you think it would be?"

"Oh my god," she says, "I think I know. You want me to take one last selfie with Kourtney while she's alive. Oh my god, it'll get so many likes. Oh my god, I just had a great idea. When you kill her, can I take a selfie with her after too? Has that like ever been done? I'll be the first. I so totally feel like Lance Armstrong before he went to the sun or whatever.

"Dear God..." I'm sure that all celestial bodies are now weeping along with me.

"Like, you know what else I'm going to do when I get out of here? I'm so getting an I Survived Killing the Kardashians shirt. Can you imagine how much money I'll make when I sell them, too?"

"Shut up, just shut the fuck up." A man has limits. Even me.

I walk towards Kim and pick her up, then set her own across from Kourtney. I get behind Kim and place the gun in her hand. I keep control of her hands so the gun remains pointed at Kourtney, who has more hate in her eyes than I've ever seen.

"I left out one important detail," I say in her ear. "You're going to have to kill Kourtney."

"Um, like what?" mumbles Kim.

"If you want the vote to hold up you're going to have to kill Kourtney. You'll have to pull the trigger."

"Just do it, Kim," says Kourtney. "If you don't he'll just kill both of us."

"Okay, sorry Kourt," says Kim.

"It's okay, just do it." My, what a good sport.

Kim is about to pull the trigger but something stops her. "Oh my god, wait!"

Kourney sighs. "You have to do it, Kim. It's me or both of us."

"So obv, but that's not it. You're wearing my shoes!"

"Fucking shoot her!" I shout it directly into her ear, wondering when I got so weary.

"Uh, hello? I will but get those shoes, please. I don't want like blood and stuff on them."

"Fuck, fine!" I take the gun from Kim and walk towards Kourtney to take her shoes. Then I throw them across the room.

Kim's mouth gapes like a fish. "Like oh my God, why did you *do* that?"

"Shut the motherfucking fuck up, I say. I get behind her again and put the gun back in her hand.

Kim points it at Kourtney, puts her finger on the trigger, and stops yet again. "Oh my God, like, I can't do it."

"I knew you had a heart, Kim," said Kourtney. "Maybe we all need to die together."

"Uh, like what?" says Kim. "No! I'm so not dying. I just can't do it because I totally realized something.

"What is it now?" I feel like someone has filled my head with broken glass.

"I can't kill her like this because she totally looks like me. I mean it's so obv that she isn't as pretty as me, but she does look a lot like me."

"Oh my God, Kim!" says Kourtney.

"What? You're not as pretty as me, but you're prettier than every other woman because you look like the cheap version of me. The cheap version of me is better than the best version of anyone else."

"That's not what I'm oh-my-God-ing about!"

"Listen to me, you fucking idiots. I have had it. You're going to blow your stupid fucking sister's brains out right now or I'll blow your brains out."

"Okay, okay," says Kim, but then she stops again. "Like I'm sorry but I'm having an issue with this."

"It's okay, I don't blame you,' says Kourtney. "You have to do it."

"Yeah like, not that. Um, it's just I keep seeing myself in you, just, you know, not as good. So like, can you get me a mirror so I can see myself when I do it? I think I might freak out seeing the not as good version of myself being killed. Like, I might think it's me for a second. Also, it's been over eight hours since my last selfie, so I've kind of forgot what I look like. It would be nice to have a refresher."

I take a deep breath. Perhaps my deepest ever. Deep like the Marianas Trench. "If I get you this fucking mirror are you going to do it then? If you don't I'll kill her myself, then kill you." I am so sick of repeating myself.

"Oh totally. No biggie. I mean she kind of deserves to die because of the Nancy thing. I just don't want to get confused that it's me for a second is all."

I'm whispering and I don't even know who I'm whispering to. "Dear fucking cocksucking Christ."

I wander away from Kim leaving the gun in her hands. I know she won't shoot me. I mean, have you been paying attention? Christ. "I just... I knew they were idiots, but never... never. Fucking unbelievable."

There's a shot behind me. I rush back to find Kim moaning in pain.

"What happened?" I say.

Kim groans. "I was looking for sparkles in the gun and it like... shot me."

So it goes, Kim.

"She's going to bleed out if you don't do something," says Kourtney. "Let her go. You said she gets to live.

"I said I wouldn't kill her," I say. "I didn't have any control over that." It's not like I told her to check the gun for sparkles, although now I kind of wish I would have.

"Like, am I going to die and stuff?" says Kim.

"It appears that way, dear." Ashes to ashes. Duh to duh.

"Oh my god, no," moans Kim. Her life is almost certainly flashing before her eyes, an endless stream of selfies.

"Do something to help her," says Kourtney.

"It's out of my hands, Kourt."

"Can I have a last request or whatever?" The condemned usually get a last meal. I wonder what Kim would order and can't come up with anything.

"Yes, of course. I'm not cruel," I say.

"Please get my phone and do something for me on it."

I grab her phone from the table.

"Go to Twitter," says Kim, her voice growing weaker with every feeble word.

"What?"

"Tweet that my status is *in pain*. Then when I die put "dead" I think it's only right that I'm the one to tweet I'm dead first."

Mithras… I mean Jesus wept. "What's the e-mail?"

"Kimmy-k-is-way-hotter-than-Khloe-Kourtney-Kendra-Paris-Caitlyn-and-her-transgender-friends-and-every-other-reality-bitch-who-wishes-she-were-me-@theprettiestkardashianever.com."

Of course. "Password?"

"Kanye's-perfect-bitch-and-I'm-like-way-prettier-than-Beyoncé-duh-and-my-vagina-looks-better-than-Khloe's-even-though-her-vagina-looks-better-than-I-thought-it-would. Oh-and-Paris-Hilton's-eyes-are-too-close-together."

I pretend to enter the insipid e-mail and password. "Okay, it looks like we're done."

"Like, totally thanks. I can die now. Wait, Kourt! If you make it out alive can you tell one of my kids… um the girl one… yeah, the girl. That one, can you tell her one thing for me, please?"

"That you love her?" says Kourtney.

I doubt that whatever she says next is going to be that thoughtful.

"Oh, um, yeah, sure. But tell her when she takes a selfie to always be facing the light. If not it creates unflattering shadows and like even at her age wrinkles might show."

Just what every girl needs to know. This is what passes for critical information these days.

Kim's head falls back and she dies or so I think. She raises her head up once more and with one last gasp she says, "Oh and I'm still prettier than Beyoncé." Now she's dead.

43

Kourtney enters a bit of a fugue state, which gives me time to think about what to do next. The show is nearly at its end and I'm surprised to find that I'm struggling with it. Not quite ready for the curtain to fall yet.

Kourtney rejoins the land of the living. "Are you like going to let me go... or..."

I watch her for a moment, then several more, then the silence stretches until she squirms. "Do you know what the most hilarious thing of all is?" I say.

"I don't think we have the same sense of humor."

I swat this comment away like a fly.

"I hate all of you because you're exactly what I've always wanted to be. The difference is I deserve to be famous because I actually have talent."

"So it is just about the fame?"

"When I was a kid I wanted to be the next Freddie Mercury with just a dash of Jim Morrison and David Bowie. Then when I got older I realized I could be better than all of them."

"I don't like understand. What does this have to do with us?"

"Our society is a moronic disposable society. You and your sisters might not be the foundation of this idiotic society, but you are the centerpiece. It's more than that though. I despise that mankind was even born. We are a complete waste in every possible way. The fact that I have to get up day after day and do the things I need to do is awful enough. We shit, piss, fuck, and vomit. We are wretched and idiotic creatures. We should be past such filth as a society, but we're not. However, the one saving grace we have as a species is art. We have the ability to create endless beauty through art. Unfortunately, we also have the ability to create endless stupidity. Most people create the latter. You, Kourtney... you're a perfect example of that. To make it even worse you've actually found a way to make a living doing it. You're atrocious and I hate you more than I've ever hated anyone or anything in my life. You and your sisters have suppressed true art in every way. However, you're going to redeem yourself with my help. You'll serve as a new form of art. Your blood will be my ink, your screams will be my poetry, and your stupidity will forever be my antagonist."

"Wow, like I'm so... sorry, but you're like totally even more of a psychopath than I ever thought. But please. Just let me go. I want to go home to my kids and I promise you I'll never do another show or interview as long as I live."

I let out a tired laugh and find myself crawling back into my thoughts. A certain song comes to mind for some reason. I take out my phone. I'm not even sure why I brought it. However, I'm glad that I did for the music I have on it. I play the song '39 by Queen. I remember at 18 before I left for college I drove to the home I once lived in with my mother before she died. On the way I listened to '39 and it moved me in a way no other song ever has. I don't remember the exact meaning of the song, but I'll try to sum it up the best I can. More or less it's about men who volunteer to explore space. They've only aged a year during the exploration. However, due to time dilation they're actually gone for a hundred years. When they return to Earth everyone they knew and loved is now dead. Their loved ones waited for them to return, but they never did in their lifetime. It's a beautiful song by Brian May. So beautiful it took me nine years to be ready to listen to it again. Anyway, when I arrived at the home I spent the first few years of my life in with my mother it looked like no one had been there in a hundred years. I forced my way in and walked around the house. I tried to imagine my mother holding me, loving me, and doing whatever it is mothers do. As I entered the master bedroom I caught the faintest essence of her. For the first time I could remember I wept. But I didn't weep because I thought of the life I could have had or a mother I once had. I wept because in that moment it was more evident than ever that I truly feel nothing. I was weeping for what I was incapable of feeling. A longing I've had all my life. Nabokov would refer to it as toska. "A sensation of great spiritual anguish, often without any specific cause." My tears were a reminder of who and what I've always been. I feel enough to care that I don't feel more, but I don't feel enough to have the ability to change it. Very much how I felt with Elizabeth. Self-awareness at its highest, yet most pathetic form. It was in that moment that I decided to fully embrace who and what it is I'm meant to be. After this realization I gathered myself and doused the home in gasoline and set it alight. I smiled as I watched it burn for a moment. Then, I got in my car and drove away without looking back even for a second. In that moment Eric Ryder was born. I had to destroy what little bit of humanity was left in me.

When I did that I was free. So, here I am listening to that song once again. Perhaps because I know it's the song that set me free the first time. Well, now it can set me free once more.

I lean over in the chair, still holding onto my gun. I stand up and move towards Kourtney. I untie her. She reluctantly stands up. She doesn't know what to do.

"What do you say?" I say, almost surprised to hear myself speaking. I hold out my hand. Nothing ventured, nothing gained and all that.

"Um, what are we doing?"

"Do you want out of this house?"

Kourtney nods and slowly takes my hand. Her fingers feel like sweaty grubs.

"At least you have some honor."

"I sure do, wifey."

"Wifey?"

"I plan to honor our vows."

I pull Kourtney against my chest and holds the gun to her head.

"Oh my God," she says.

"What do you say? Let's go out like Bonnie and Clyde." I laugh wildly. I realize that if I don't stop, I'll never be able to quell it again. Oh well.

"Please, please, no."

"Say, if I shoot at them and use you as a shield, do you think they'll shoot back at me? I've always wondered... Let's find out."

I open the door, facing the police as Kourtney screams. I begin dragging her through the door and into the police lights.

"Waterman!" I'm screaming. "Aim for my face! Pretend I'm Kris Jenner..."

When they create a religion in my honor instead of being nailed to a cross I'll be nailed to a cell phone being forced to use social media. I turned water into blood. I healed society of its blindness. I wasn't born of a virgin; I was born of a dead woman. I didn't just walk on water I fucking ran on it while pissing just for good measure. Fuck your Christ. I'm your Ryder.

Flowing from entwine in the devouring light as this ~~Momentary Glamour Messiah.~~ No, that's not right. Flowing from entwine in the devouring light as this Eternal. Glamour. Messiah.

THE END

* 9 7 8 0 6 9 2 8 0 2 8 2 3 *